ROUGAROU IV
SHADOWS OF THE PAST

JUDITH ANN MCDOWELL

This is a work of fiction. Names, characters, places, and incidents are products of the author's imagination or are used fictitiously and are not to be construed as real. Any resemblance to actual events, locations, organizations, or persons, living or dead, is entirely coincidental.

World Castle Publishing, LLC
Pensacola, Florida
Copyright © Judith Ann McDowell 2021
Paperback ISBN: 9781955086264
eBook ISBN: 9781955086271
First Edition World Castle Publishing, LLC, 05/22/2021
http://www.worldcastlepublishing.com
Licensing Notes
Cover: Karen Fuller

DEDICATION

Jill Breivik Hersey, for giving me the idea for Jillianna Romanitti.

CHAPTER 1

Saint Anthony Parish, Louisiana 2017

Her wet mouth moves over his hot skin, making his breath come faster as he entangles a hand in her long blond hair to yank her mouth upward.

"I knew you would come back to me, Karleto," she whispers. Her blue-green eyes, filled with a hint of self-satisfied smugness, stare into his

"Don't talk," he panted. "I don't want to hear your voice." His probing tongue tastes the sweetness of her open mouth. "I only want to feel the touch of your skin on mine."

She smiles, running her sharp red nails over his chest.

He moans deep in his throat at the feel of her long, slender legs straddling his body. He hears a taunting laugh escape her throat as his mouth moves over the throbbing pulse of her neck, then lower to her full breasts.

"We belong together, you and I," she breathes, fisting a handful of his thick, black hair as she rubs herself roughly against his rock-hard need. "Now, you will see this."

"No!" He screams the word, flailing his arms as he sits bolt upright in the bed.

"Jack," Seelah turns over in the bed, and reaching out, draws him into her arms. "You were having a bad dream."

"Yes." He leans away, running a shaking hand over his sweating face.

"Can you tell me what the dream was about? If you can, maybe I can find out why..." she inhales a deep breath as she stares at him. "Do you know the blond-haired woman who was with you in your dream?"

Her soothing voice takes on a biting edge now.

Jack throws back the covers to get to his feet. "A person can't help what they dream, Seelah." His tone is cutting.

Her dark brown eyes skim over his nakedness, admiring the taut muscles of his slim, toned body, but as her gaze moves down over his aroused manhood, she feels her jealousy rise. "You know who this woman is, Jack. Do not lie to my face."

Jack stomps past her to the bathroom. "This is what comes of havin' a psychic for a wife," he murmurs under his breath.

"Yes, Jack, this is what happens when a man has a psychic for a wife." Seelah bounds out of bed to stand with her hands balled on her slim hips. Wearing a pale blue satin nightie with a built-in bra, her small breasts rise and fall now with her anger, giving her the appearance of an angry teenager.

She raises her voice to be heard as Jack continues on his way down the hall. "And don't think we are through discussing this vivid dream."

Stepping into the shower stall, Jack leans forward, turning the tap all the way over to cold. The icy spray hits his sweating body like a bolt of liquid fire. Lifting the handheld shower head straight upward, he allows the stinging mist to beat his throbbing head as he tries not to think of the beautiful woman who laughed and taunted him in his nighttime wanderings. The woman he knows as Jillianna Romanitti.

Dressed now in a pair of jeans and a lightweight sweatshirt, Jack walks into the small dining room to seat himself in a chair pulled back away from the table. He brings the cup of coffee Seelah sat before him up to his mouth in hopes the steaming liquid will chase away the last of the cobwebs from his mind.

"I apologize for being angry earlier, Jack. I guess seeing a beautiful woman lying nude in bed with my husband caught me off guard. But, you're right. You can't help what you dream."

Jack concentrated on keeping his eyes cast downward.

Seelah watches him, then turns away.

They both look up at Donny, their five-year-old, as he walks into the room.

Feeling as though he has been handed a reprieve, Jack grins as he pulls the young boy over to him.

"What are your plans for this sunny spring Saturday, Son?

Seelah smiles, gazing at her two favorite males. With their heads close together, they looked so much alike she feels her heart swell with overflowing love.

"Do you think we could go and visit Uncle Donavan and Aunt Barbara and Jenny? That's always fun."

"I'm sure we can find out real quick." Jack turns to pull his cell phone from the charger at the end of the counter. He punches in some numbers and then waits as the number rings. As he hears the voice of his best friend and partner pick up on the other line, he hands the phone to Donny.

"Hi, Uncle Donavan, it's me, Donny, calling to talk with you."

Donny laughs and then holds the phone against his chest.

"Uncle Donavan said I just made his day."

Jack reaches out, taking the phone. "Hey Donavan, hope we didn't catch you at a bad time. When I asked Donny what he wants to do today, he said he wants to visit you guys. So, do you have any plans you can't break?"

Jack laughs aloud, watching the serious look on his son's face.

"Okay, we'll be over after breakfast. We'll figure out what we can do after we all get together."

"I take it Donavan and Barb don't have any plans that can possibly keep them from spending the day with the Olivier's." Seelah's dark brown head turns to look at them as she lifts a bottle of Orange Juice from the refrigerator.

The spurt of laughter erupting from Jack's throat lifts away the last of his bad feelings. "You know as well as I if they do, they'll shelve them for the chance to spend the day with their favorite half-pint."

"I hope Jenny's gonna spend the day with us, too. I like bein' round her," Donny said.

"I'm sure she will. I think Jenny likes bein' `round you as much as you like bein' `round her." Jack ruffles the top of Donny's dark brown head. "For a fifteen-year-old, I'd say Jenny has her act pretty much together. Unlike most of the teens walkin' `round these days."

"I agree. Jenny is a very nice young lady," Seelah speaks up. I think the terrible ordeal she suffered when she was younger made her mature a lot faster than most girls her age."

"Did someone hurt Jenny, Mama?" Donny asked, his brow creasing with anger.

"It ain't anything you need to concern yourself with, Son. Mama spoke `fore she thought's all.

"Yes, I did. Jenny is a good girl and one we are all proud of."

"I think she's a good girl, too." Donny's olive-complexioned face turns a slight shade of red as he voices his feelings.

"We all love our Jenny, Donny," Seelah tells him, turning away before Donny could see the slight grin she could not control over her son's first crush.

"If we're gonna spend the day with our family up the block, we better get a move on with breakfast." Jack chuckles.

Seelah sits quietly eating her food; however, her mind is on the strange dream in which her husband had been a pawn in the arms of a beautiful woman. Jack was right in saying a person is not responsible for his dreams. None the less she had a feeling this dream was more than a mere cleansing of the mind as dreams were prone to be.

CHAPTER 2

Jillianna Romanitti stands looking out over her well-manicured lawns. A sheer, sea green Caftan covers her nude body. Catching her reflection in the window, she smiles at the beautiful woman looking back at her.

She glories in the knowledge that the Romanitti name is still respected by many people even though she now makes her home in the subtropical climate of Louisiana instead of the cool temperatures of her native-born Romania. And, too, knowing that the Romanitti Family has always enjoyed the ever envious privilege of being born into massive wealth, living in beautiful mansions, and knowing the clothes on their back fashions the best names in the business.

She smiles, thinking about all her vast wealth can bring to her at a moment's notice, such as waking up in the middle of the night with a strong desire to share her bed with a beautiful young woman. She knows she needs only to pick up her phone and order up her preference. If her craving is for that of a handsome young man to make love with her throughout the long night, she has but to send Baxter, who knows her preference, to find this young man, and bring him here to the mansion.

And yet, she remains unfulfilled. She knows the man who can still the hunger burning within her body and mind is a man she cannot have, and this knowing leaves her body wanting more.

She turns as Baxter enters the room dressed in a pair of black pants and a white shirt and carrying a tray holding a filled glass and a cup filled with steaming liquid.

"I'll have my tomato juice and coffee on the patio this morning, Baxter. It is a beautiful morning, and I feel like being out in the open."

"Yes'm, I'll bring that out to you right away."

Jillianna smiles as Baxter turns to leave. "I am glad you have chosen to stay with me through all these years, Baxter. I would miss you terribly if you were not with me."

"Don't you worry none 'bout that, Ms. Jillianna. Ain't no place I'd rather be than right here with you." Baxter looks at her, his aged and black skin creasing into a wide grin.

On the patio, she pulls her pale blond, waist-length hair over one shoulder and then stretches her well-developed body out straight on a chase lounge. As she sips at her chilled glass of juice, she thinks about her time spent in the arms of her night-time lover.

She can still feel his hands on her body. Feel his hot mouth move over her skin.

She plucks a piece of ice from her glass, putting it into her mouth to collect the juice with her tongue, before moving the frozen cube over the throbbing pulse, making itself known on the side of her neck.

The face of Karleto, her handsome gypsy lover from centuries past, moves into her mind making her pulse throb with the memory. A woman always remembers her first love and the first man to change her body from the innocence of youth to the passionate needs of a grown woman.

Jillianna brings the face of Jack Olivier' to the forefront of her mind and compares the two men who bring out the volatile cravings of a libido too hot to be ignored.

She can see so much likeness in these two men who share the same soul. Almost mirror images of one another except Jack's personality is that of a more volatile nature that, when aroused, can burst forth into an all-out explosion. This knowing intensifies her need for him

Tired of fighting her body's needs, she gives into them on a nightly basis. In the late hours of the night, she sets her spirit free to go to the man, whom she believes can still the overpowering hunger calling out to be satisfied. With his subconscious mind free of outside concerns, it is easy for her spirit to enter into his relaxed state, thus allowing him to interact with his own aroused desires. Believing, all the while, it is only an innocent dream.

With her own needs growing stronger due to Jack's refusal to surrender to her prowess, Jillianna knows she will have to find someone to take the edge off her hunger.

The thought of Jack belonging to another woman, who can share his desires without his holding back, is enough to set her anger spewing forth into a white-hot rage. He must belong to her and to her alone. She cannot be satisfied with another lover. Only Karleto, living now in the body of Jack, can bring out her passion and douse the fires burning out of control in her hungry body.

As always happened, when her body has been left overlong without being sated, her hunger for the sweet red blood running through the veins of a beautiful, young woman nags at her. To appease this need, she turns to her second choice.

Getting to her feet, Jillianna walks into the living room to remove a folded leather bag from a small drawer in an end table.

Seating herself on a white leather couch, she opens the bag to withdraw a small razor-sharp dagger along with a bottle of rubbing alcohol and some cotton balls.

Rolling up the sleeve of her Caftan, she takes the dagger in her hand to make a small cut across her wrist. As the blood rushes to the surface, she brings the open wound up to her waiting mouth. Her eyes close on the sensual feelings, making themselves known as the sweet nectar runs down her throat.

Jillianna leans back against the couch. Her breathing is deep and relaxing, allowing her to bask in the feelings her mind and body are enjoying.

Her mind slips back to the past when she was still able to enjoy her time with her gypsy lover, Karleto.

Dressed in a dark green day dress, her long blond hair fanned out around her, Jillianna lays on her back in the sweet-smelling grass.

"My beautiful Jillianna," the deep voice of Karleto whispered.

"We should not be here together like this, but I cannot stay away from you. If my father finds out I am spending time alone with a man, instead of safe in the castle surrounded by love ones, he can have me killed for the shame I would bring on the name of Romanitti."

"You must come away with me. We will travel far so no one in my band will be blamed for our being together." Karleto ran a hand over her blond hair, and leaning forward, brushed a tender kiss across her full mouth.

"My father would not stop at spilling the blood of only your band, Karleto. His rage would be out of control. He is a very proud man, my father. The thought of his being bested by a mere gypsy would further his anger."

The tone of her words made Karleto lean back to glare at her.

"Do these feelings own your heart, too, Jillianna? My being a mere gypsy?"

For a moment, she looked away, thinking on his words, then smiled. "No, Karleto, your gypsy blood does not lessen my love for you. I am saying what feelings would enter into my father's heart."

"Your blood is pure. The Romanitti name is spoken with much respect and awe in this land." Karleto sat up then got to his feet. This is why your father makes sure you will remain untouched until the night of your wedding." He turns away as anger at the thought of another man touching his Jillianna twist his features into an ugly scowl.

"I fear if I am unable to stay away from you, I will bring much danger to those of my blood. We have been raised to think of others before thinking of ourselves."

"Then you must be the strong one, my Karleto. I will leave now. If I do not go out alone in search of you, you will find another." She rose to her feet, and with one last look at the handsome young man who stood watching her, she ran quickly back in the direction of the castle.

Jillianna sets forward, allowing the sad memory in her mind to fade. However, the hot need running through her body at seeing her lover cannot be so easily stilled.

CHAPTER 3

Donny laughs aloud as Jenny gives him a big hug.

"My favorite little brother. I'm glad we're gonna be spending the entire day together here at the amusement park."

"Me too, Jenny. Do you really look at me like your little brother?"

"You're the closest to a little brother as I'm ever gonna have. And even if I were to get a brother, he sure couldn't take your place in my feelings."

"No one can ever take your place in my feelings either, Jenny." Donny's eyes are adoring as he gazes at Jenny.

Seelah nudges Barbara to follow her gaze across the way.

"Okay, what are you two hatching up?" Donavan walks over to where Seelah and Barbara stand talking. "We came here to have a good time. Even Brandy and Lugar are happy to be here, smelling all the good smells and seeing all the people milling around."

"I'm glad there are places we can take our four-legged babies." She reaches out, patting the heads of both dogs, laughing as she receives a quick lick on the hand in return. "Remember when we were all having lunch on the patio at one of the restaurants, and we had Brandy and Lugar with us?"

"Oh yeah, Barb. You're talking about the day we had the misfortune to run into Lawrence Hindel and his flavor of the day," Donavan laughs. "I thought Jack was going to put a bullet in Lawrence's honey. He was that mad."

"What the hell, could you blame me?" Jack growled, walking forward to pull Seelah against his hip. "The son-of-a-bitch caught me off guard to throw a fist in my face."

"All the Hindels are evil," Seelah whispers, turning to wrap her arms around Jack's waist and lay her head on his chest.

"I never thought I would live to see the things we've seen in our lifetime, and most of it is right here in our own parish."

"Please," Jenny murmurs. "Can we not talk about the Hindels?

Barbara drapes an arm over Jenny's shoulder and gives her a hug. "I'm sorry, sweetheart. I didn't see you standing there."

"Mama said you had a bad thing happen, Jenny. No one had better try'n hurt you while I'm around," Donny walks forward and takes one of Jenny's hands in his.

"Aw, thank you, Donny. I love you so much." Jenny gives his hand a quick squeeze.

"Okay, that all happened some time ago. We are all safe, and we will remain safe," Donavan says, grinning as he watches Jenny and Donny walk off together. "We need to pay closer attention to what we say when Jenny is around. I don't want her to start having nightmares again."

"Let's hope that all that mess that lived here before is over and done with. All the Hindels are dead and gone, so we should be able to live a happy life here in the parish from now on. But, didn't you say we have a vampire living in our midst now? What is her name? Romanitti or something strange like that," Barbara says, looking over at Donavan.

"Yeah, Jillianna Romanitti. She said she's from Romania. Guess that explains the reason she is a vampire. Must be related to Dracula." His voice slips into an alluring, Romanian brogue as he pronounces each syllable of the name. "I have to admit, though, she is one good-looking woman." Donavan snickers, giving Barbara a quick wink.

"What does she look like, Donavan?" Seelah looks directly at him.

"If we're gonna make a day of it, we need to get a move on. Standin' here talkin' 'bout werewolves and vampires is a waste of good sunlight." Jack takes hold of Seelah's hand. "Come on, kids." He swings an arm in a wide arch. "We're finally gettin' this crowd on the road to havin' some fun."

Donavan gives Jack a quick glance, his brows raised, then turns to follow the rest as they move off.

"Okay, now that we're here, we need to decide what we want to do first." Barbara smiles as Donny reaches for Jenny's hand.

"I think we should get some cotton candy," Donny piped up.

"We can do that," Barbara looks around at the others.

"I'll pass. I'm happy being the new heartthrob of Saint Anthony Parish." Donavan pats his all but flat stomach.

"All right, Handsome, we'll take that as a no." Barbara laughs as Donavan spins around, showing off his trim physique. "Jack?" Barbara looks over at him.

"I'm gonna pass. Too early in the day to be havin' any sweets." Jack reaches into his back pocket for his wallet.

"I'm getting this one," Barbara tells him.

Jack pushes his wallet back down in the pocket of his jeans and then glances up as he feels Donavan nudge him and signal him off to the side.

"What the hell's going on with you and Seelah?"

"What do you mean?"

"What do I mean? If you could have seen your face when I mentioned Jillianna Romanitti and what a looker she is, you wouldn't be asking. Your face blanched as white as a shaker of salt."

Jack quickly glanced at the Little Cotton Candy Hut, where Seelah and Barbara and the kids are standing together. "I'll catch you up later. For now, let's just concentrate on enjoyin' our get-together with the family."

For a moment, Donavan continues to look at him, then, seeing the others coming towards them, he glances away.

For the rest of the afternoon, the two families enjoy playing games, taking rides on the merry go round and even being daring enough to chance the heart-stopping thrill of the fast-moving roller coaster. They end their day filling up on the great foods the midway has to offer.

Jack, Seelah and Donny have just walked into the house when Jack's cell phone goes off.

"I knew our luck with havin' a good day was too good to hold," Jack said, pulling his cell phone from the holder on his belt. "Yeah?"

"Why don't you meet me back here, and we can sit out in the backyard with a beer?" Donavan's voice comes to him on the other line.

"Sounds right." Jack glanced up to see Seelah watching him from across the room. "Any sign of a forced entry?"

"I take it Seelah is nearby."

"That would be my guess."

"Then, instead of you coming here, I'll roll by and pick you up, and we can go to the station. This way, no lies will be told, and we won't have to field Barb's questions why Seelah and Donny didn't come back with you."

"Sounds good. See ya in a few."

Jack shuts off his phone and hangs the phone back on his belt. "That was Donavan. Somethin's come up. He's gonna roll by for me in a few minutes. Sorry, Baby. I knew this day was goin' too good."

"You are a detective, Jack. A detective has no days off. Maybe Donny and I will walk up to visit with Barb and Jenny. No use sitting here by ourselves."

"Good idea. So, when we get done at the station, I'll just go on home with Donavan."

Seelah giggles. "As much time as all of us spend together, I don't know why we don't all live in one big house."

Jack walks over to her and, taking her into his arms, brushes a kiss down the side of her face. "I like havin' our home to ourselves, Seelah."

Seelah leans back to gaze up at him. "I am sorry for being angry with you earlier, Jack. I don't mean to be jealous of you. I know with your job you are bound to meet beautiful women. And, too, as you said, you can't help what you dream.

Jack pulls her back into his arms and is happy when he hears the honking of a car horn telling him Donavan has arrived to pick him up.

"My love for you and our son will never change, Seelah. You are the woman I love, and I always will."

Walking outside, he nods to Donavan as he sits behind the wheel, watching him. Jack pulls open the car door to slide inside.

"Okay, what is going on that you need my help this time?"

"Let's get outta here. I feel like a cheatin' piece of shit."

"You're telling me you cheated on Seelah?" Donavan laughs outright. "When, in your dreams? That's the only time you could, the rest of the time you're with me."

When Jack remains silent, Donavan backs the jeep out of the driveway.

"Do you still want to go to the station?"

"I told Seelah we were goin' to the station, so yes, I want to go to the station." Jack's voice takes on an icy tone. "I've already told her enough lies. I don't need to pack on anymore."

They ride in silence until Donavan pulls the jeep into the parking space in front of the sheriff's station and turns off the key. Without a word, they walk into the station.

"Hey, Lieutenant," a uniformed officer behind the desk speaks up. "I was just about to call you."

"Oh yeah. About what?"

"A young girl's body was found out at the Old Hindel Mansion. Thought since all the Hindels were done away with, we wouldn't have to worry about all this anymore."

"How long ago did it happen?" The man behind the desk has his attention now.

"I got a call in at 5:32 PM about some rowdy teens being on the property. I sent out two uniforms. They didn't find any teens. I didn't think it was important to call you right away since the Hindels aren't there anymore..." the dispatcher's voice trails off as he sees the look of anger spreading across his Lieutenant's face.

"Did you get the name of the caller?"

"No, Sir. A man said he was calling to report a bunch of rowdy teens being on Hindel Property. Thought we should send someone to check it out."

"So, he wasn't calling about a dead girl on the estate?"

"No, Sir. Not at first. He was concerned about teens being on the place. Just before you came into the station, he called back to say there was a dead girl in the driveway."

"Are the uniforms still on the property?"

"Yes, Sir, they are."

"Radio them to stay on the scene and let them know Detective Olivier' and I are on our way out there."

"Yes, Sir, Lieutenant Hays."

"Seelah said she was gonna take Donny and go back to your house. I'll call and let her know we may be a while."

"Good idea."

Jack pulls his cell phone from his belt and punches in the numbers to the Hays' home phone.

"Hey, Barb, it's Jack. Has Seelah made it to your house yet? Good. Yeah, if I could, thanks." Jack waits while Seelah comes to the phone.

"Hey Baby, just wanted to let you know Donavan and I are gonna be longer than we thought. We just got a call about a young girl found dead out at the Old Hindel Mansion."

"Let's go, Jack. Tell her we'll be back as soon as we can."

"Gotta go, Baby. Love ya." Jack clicks off his cell.

***

Seelah hangs up the phone and then stands thinking about what Jack has told her about a girl being found dead on Hindel Property.

"What is going on, Seelah? You look upset."

"I am upset, Barb. Jack called to tell me they will be gone longer than they thought. Seems a girl's body was found out at the old Hindel Mansion."

"Oh god. Not again. I thought we were through with all the evil that place sends out."

"So did I. Someone needs to put a torch to that house and burn it to the ground. With all the Hindels dead and in hell, this time, there would be no one else to rebuild like Lawrence did."

"Who called in about the body?"

Seelah looked at her. "That is a good question, Barb. A question we need to find the answer to."

***

"I swear to Christ, I could open this door and puke. We were through with the Hindels. This parish and its people don't need this filth startin' all over again.

"I hear ya, Jack. I remember you saying when we thought we were done with the Hindels that the next one to move into the mansion might be a vampire." Donavan looked over at him. "Which reminds me. You were going to tell me what had you so ready to kick your own ass for being a cheating cad."

"I've been havin' strange dreams for the past few weeks."

"Okay, how does this filter into your being a cheater?"

"I'm not in my dreams alone, Donavan." Jack glances at him and then looks away.

"I would sure as hell hope not if you feel you're being a cheater. Otherwise, all that's going on is your hands aren't being idle while you're in dreamville."

"I'm not havin' a dream 'bout jerkin' off, Donavan." Jack's voice shot into the silence. "I'm dreamin' bout havin' sex with a woman other than Seelah."

Donavan laughed outright. "You're having what is called, by know-all-see-all head doctors, a wet dream. At your age, I'm surprised you never had the pleasure."

"Don't be a wise-ass, Donavan. Of course, I've had wet

dreams. This dream's different. There's no problem with Seelah and me in the love department. Wet dreams are for those dissatisfied assholes who have a wife who won't put out, or they don't have the price of a hooker."

"Hmm, I never thought about it from that angle before, but you could have a valid point. What makes you think this dream is different?" Donavan tries to keep a straight face, knowing Jack is not in a joking mood.

"The woman is the same in all the dreams." Jack wipes a hand across his sweating brow. "So far, I haven't finished the act, but I have to admit, I've come damn close."

"Maybe you just solved the problem. Finish the act, and the dream will go away."

"This morning, I screamed out in my sleep. Scared the hell outta Seelah. She was tryin' to comfort me until she suddenly zeroed in on what I was dreamin' 'bout and with who."

"So, what you're saying is Seelah knows you are having dreams about another woman. Does the woman say anything in the dream that can tell you who she is?"

"She doesn't need to say anything for me to know who she is. The woman in my dream is Jillianna Romanitti."

CHAPTER 4

"Same fuckin' lane leadin' up to the same fuckin' locked gate."

"At least this time, the gate is open. This has to mean someone is in the house whose knowledgeable in how the electrical gate panel works.

"Yeah, now the question is who?" Jack shakes a cigarette out of the package before pulling his lighter from the holder on his belt. "I'll tell you right now. If I see one more Hindel walk through that door, you better get ready to back me cause I swear to Christ, I'll empty all six rounds into the son of a bitch.

Donavan braked the jeep in back of the two police cars parked in front of the mansion. "I hear you. I feel the same way."

"You'd think if they can redo this place, they could get someone new to move in."

"This whole place is filled with evil. They can never get rid of that even if they were to torch it along with every blade of grass around it."

As Donavan and Jack stepped out of the jeep, two sheriff deputies walk down the steps of the front porch.

"Looks like we're about to find out what's going on," Donavan says.

"Lieutenant Hays, Jack." One of the deputies holds out a hand as he walks forward.

"Brewster. I take it you're the one who opened the gate?"

"No, Sir. The gate was already open when we got here."

Jack turned and walked over to the nude body of a young girl lying on her back just off the driveway. He could see her throat had been ripped out.

"Brewster, go get the camera off the back seat," Jack said.

"We can already tell this killing was not done by a human," Donavan says as he stands looking at the mutilated body.

"Hell no, it wasn't done by a human. It's the same damn M.O. as the rest of the killin's we've seen involvin' this pig sty."

"Here ya go, Sir," the deputy says, holding the camera by a wide strap attached at both ends.

"Thanks, Brewster."

"How much of the house did you check out before we got here?" Donavan moves away as Jack snaps off pictures of the body.

Donavan noticed the look passing between the two deputies and knew he already had his answer.

"Don't feel too bad. This goddamn place gives everybody the heebee jeebies."

"This is my first time comin' out here. Although, like everyone else in the parish, I've heard all the stories about what is supposed to go on out here, this is the first time I've seen it for myself. Guess the stories weren't so far off after all."

"Brewster, you ain't heard half of what's gone on in this place. I could tell you things that would make you piss your pants, and it wouldn't even be the worst of what Lieutenant Hays and

I've been privy to."

"That's all right, Jack. I'd rather not go into all the grisly details." Brewster backs away. "I've got three youngin's, and from what I have heard about this place, little kids is what gets preyed upon."

"We may as well get it over with and go inside. This way, maybe we can tell if someone is living here." Donavan takes his camera from Jack and, moving over to the jeep, lays the camera back on the seat.

"Come on, you and your partner can go inside with us," Jack stifles the grin lifting the corners of his full mouth at the look on the other man's face. "This place calls for extra backup. One thing you need to remember. You don't ever come to this house alone. I don't care if it's in the middle of the day or the middle of the night. You stay outside the gate with your piece unholstered until backup arrives."

"Jack's right. You may not believe all the stories, but suffice it to say, The Hindel Mansion is not a place you want to play with."

Both deputies walked slowly behind the two detectives up the wide stone steps to the front porch and into the mansion.

Standing in the huge, well-furnished kitchen, they look around at all the wealth surrounding them.

"Top of the line appliances, you have to admit that. The Hindels spare no expense when it comes to making sure they have the best."

"Yeah, and can you believe Lawrence Hindel didn't even go to the furniture store and pick out what he wanted to furnish this place with? He called the store and told them what he wanted," Jack said. "Then, to top it off, not long after the furniture was delivered, the owner of the store was found dead in his bed with his throat tore out. Hmm, I guess it could be a coincidence that right now we have a young girl layin' out in the driveway with her throat tore out, too, but for some reason, I don't think so."

"Then what you're sayin' is, you believe all those cockamamie stories about the Hindels bein' Rougarous or werewolves or whatever they are said to be?" The deputy's voice drips sarcasm.

At the same time, both Donavan and Jack turn to look at the deputy standing beside Brewster, and without a word, they break out in a fit of laughter.

"I guess we can take that to mean the stories are true, partner," Brewster grinned, slapping the other man on the shoulder.

"I know we've all been brought up to believe that werewolves and vampires exist only in the imagination of writers, but I can say in all honesty, I have yet to meet a Hindel who ain't into dancin' with the devil."

"Okay, let's get busy checking out the rest of this shithole. Maybe if we get lucky, we'll get to put a bullet in one of these devil dancing fuckers." Donavan said.

"Hello?" A female voice calls out into the silence.

All four men stop.

"Who the hell could that be?" Donavan said. "Did one of you already call the coroner? Maybe she's an assistant M.E."

"No, we thought it best to wait until you got here to say what to do," Brewster delivered.

"Well, we're not gonna find out who she is standin' here talkin'." Jack turns around on the stairs.

At that moment, a very beautiful young woman walks inside the mansion. "Hello?"

Jack moved back down the staircase. "What is your name, and what business do you have at this residence, Miss?"

The woman looked at him with a questioning look on her face, her blue-green eyes becoming hostile. "I could ask you the same question, boy. I am Regina Hindel, and this is my estate."

Jack stands motionless, staring at the woman as though he has seen a ghost, and wondering why.

"Are you going to stand there like a complete idiot, or are you going to tell me who you are and what you are doing in my house? And, what police cars are doing in my driveway?"

Donavan comes forward. "I am Detective Lieutenant Donavan Hays of the Saint Anthony Parish Sheriff's Department, and this is my partner, Detective Jack Olivier'.

"Alright, that answers part of my question, but I still want to know what you are doing here."

Donavan can see the tall, slender woman standing before him is monetarily well off. From diamond studs, peeking out from long blond hair that did not come from a bottle to her white silk blouse and black skirt offset by her black, high heeled shoes; this is a woman used to giving orders and having those orders obeyed.

"What we are doin' here is investigatin' a murder." Jack comes forward. "Case you didn't notice on your way inside your estate, there is a dead body layin' in your driveway. We'll need to see some ID, Miss."

"I have already told you my name and that this is my estate." Her sultry voice has lost none of its commanding tone.

"Yeah, well, I could say I'm Mister Green Jeans, and this is my barn, but I'd still have to show ID to prove it if the police show up at my barn to investigate a murder."

Pulling the handbag she has slung over her shoulder from

off her arm, she lifts a wallet up and out into the open. "Here," she flips the wallet open to show an ID card.

"Could you take it out of the wallet, please?" Jack stands with his hands at his side.

"I can tell you were a rookie before getting your big promotion. You probably got off on stopping unchaperoned women, just to make yourself feel good." She pulls the ID into view.

"There see, that wasn't so difficult." Jack looks down at the card. "Yep, accordin' to this, you're a Hindel, alright. You have my condolences."

"You are one of the most rude individuals I have ever had the misfortune to come across. You and your men need to get finished and get out of my house!"

"It isn't that easy, Miss Hindel." Donavan walks over to stand, looking at her. "As Detective Olivier' said, this is a murder investigation, which means this house and the surrounding area is a crime scene."

"Then get done what you have to do, and get out. I have driven from New Orleans, and I am tired."

"Again, it is not going to be that easy. Since this is a crime scene, you will need to vacate the premises until we've finished our investigation."

"You cannot be serious. This is my home, and I am telling you to take your men, and all of you get out!"

"No can do, Missy." Jack grins. "And, I think I should warn you that if you continue to impede this investigation, we will be forced to arrest you."

Her blue-green eyes flash fire as she stands glaring at him.

"I can already tell you ain't thrilled with how things are shapin' up here, but it can't be helped. Someone decided to murder a young girl on the Hindel Estate, and until we find out who that someone is, you are going to be spending your time in a hotel or motel in town. And while we are on the subject of The Hindel Estate, I am going to need to see proof that you are now the legal owner and have a right to be here."

In a huff, she wheels around to leave, then stops. "Don't any of you be surprised when you receive notice that you are being sued for not allowing me to stay in my own home."

"Okay, we've been warned," Jack tells her before turning to the two deputies standing nearby. "Brewster, you can see Miss Hindel to her car. If she gives you any problem with leaving, you are to arrest her and take her to the station."

As Brewster steps forward, Regina puts out her hands. "If you dare put your hands on me, I will sue you."

"What in the hell is it with Hindels? Every time we turned around, they were threatening to sue for some reason or other."

"We both know it went a lot further than that, partner." Jack gazes over at her as she stands glaring back at him. "If they'd just stopped at wantin' to sue, this parish wouldn't have wanted to band together and shoot the sons of bitches. But no, they had to turn into a bunch of flesh eatin', blood suckin' ghouls, and go after our children!"

"What in the name of God are you talking about?" Regina's face shows her shock at his words. "Have you gone mad? My loved ones would never do something like that."

"Yeah, well, I got a big news flash for you, baby! They not only would, they have. And I have about as much respect for anyone with the name of Hindel as I would for any other serial killer!"

"Jack, I think we need to let Miss Hindel be on her way so we can get back to work."

Regina Hindel stands looking at the men who stare back at her with a look of pure loathing covering their faces. "All right, I'll go, but you haven't heard the last of me. I am sure when I tell my relatives in New Orleans what is going on here, they will be arriving to make sure I am not mistreated."

"If any Hindels come back to this parish, they will be shot on sight. This I can promise you, Miss Hindel. Everyone who lives here thought we had heard the last of the Hindels. Now you are telling us that there are more of you still alive. We will not go through the hell that your family put this parish through. We will shoot every last one of you and burn this goddamn house to the ground if need be to keep all of you out of here," Donavan growled as he stares her down.

"I'm calling my attorney. I cannot believe what I have walked into here. All of you behave as though you have lost your senses. The Hindel name is something to be proud of, not feared."

"Goodbye, Miss Hindel. The deputies will see you on your way," Donavan tells her.

"I can't believe this is all happenin' again," Jack runs a sweaty hand down the pant leg of his jeans. "I hope she tells the ones she thinks will haul ass here to save her, what you said. This parish'll come unhinged when they hear the Hindels are alive and well and plannin' a reunion."

"I suggest we call a meeting with brass and find out exactly what our options are. I know that as much as we would like to do what I told her we would do, I don't think the higher-ups will go for our opening fire on any Hindels who come back into the parish."

They both walk to the front door as they hear a car roar off down the lane

CHAPTER 5

"I think our finding out who called in about a dead body out at the old Hindel Mansion is a great idea, and I am sure Donavan and Jack could use the information, too," Barbara said.

Seelah sat quietly as she relaxed her mind to find out what they needed to know. Within moments she sat forward.

"The person who called in was not reporting on the girl found in the driveway. He was calling about rowdy teens on the estate."

"How could he not know about a dead body? If he was on the estate, he had to have seen a body."

"We would think. But anyway, he is a white man in his middle forties. He is a very handsome man, big in stature, and he has long black hair that he keeps tied back in a ponytail. I don't get that this man is bad. He is a man who will be working on the estate. He will be living in the small cottage Lawrence Hindel had rebuilt after the old mansion and cottage were blown up."

"If this man is going to be working on the estate, then this means someone is moving back into the mansion."

"They already are. A woman."

Seelah catches her breath as she sees the woman up close. "What's wrong? You look upset."

"This morning, Jack woke from a nightmare he was having, and while I was trying to comfort him, I saw who else was in his dream. It was a woman, and she looked very much like the woman who is moving into the Hindel Mansion. Although she is not the woman in Jack's dream, she certainly looks a lot like her."

"At least this time, the grounds keeper won't be old and ugly like Mr. Quigly."

"You forgot to mention evil."

"All those years, Lawrence Hindel believed Jonathan was his father only to find out that instead of Jonathan, his father was Quigly."

"Can you blame him? I sure wouldn't want Quigly as my father. The one I felt sorry for is Chandra. The way Lawrence carried on in front of her about how ashamed he felt in finding out his mother was a black woman."

"I wish Chandra would come for a visit."

"So do I, Barbara. Chandra is a good woman."

"You say she is a good woman. Don't you mean was a good woman?"

"I say is, because Chandra is very much alive on the other side. Only our body dies. Our spirit lives on. We know who we are when we step from our body to leave this plane. Our minds are sharp no matter what age we are when we leave."

"Are you saying that even someone who was suffering from Alzheimer's Disease is coherent when they die?"

"Barbara, our bodies are only a shell. Our spirits are who we are. When we leave that shell, we no longer suffer any disease or pain. However, if we are depressed or suffer from a violent death, we may need to be put into a twilight sleep on the other side until we can understand that we are no longer in body. And in this case, a loved one will come from the other side to take us home."

"One thing I have always had a problem understanding is, why, when a person dies, do they remain on this earth?"

"Sometimes, it is not their wish to remain. Sometimes they are kept on this plane by an evil entity. And yes, there are those who choose to remain on this plane for one reason or another. Sometimes that reason is they believe they are not good enough to go home because of some wrong they have committed against God. At times, religion can be a very dangerous teaching. Some religions teach that this earth is all there is. That when you die, you are buried, and that is where you stay until The Rapture when Jesus comes back."

"Are you saying that that belief is wrong?

"I'm saying everyone is entitled to their own belief, but since I have the gift of being able to see what some cannot, I view this life in a different light."

"And what about those who are kept here by an evil entity? How do they get to go to the other side?"

"A lot of times, they can be led home by someone like me, a psychic. Other times, a priest can free them from the evil ones holding them on this plane." Seelah smiles over at her. "I like to think we are never without help."

"I like to think this, too. Now, getting back to the man who called in on the murder, I think we should let the guys find out what you know so they can be prepared."

"Good idea, Barb. Like the old saying goes, forewarned is forearmed. And when one is dealing with the Hindel Mansion, this is never more true," Seelah whispers.

***

Jack grabs his cell phone from the holder as it begins to ring. "Yeah?" He smiles as he hears Seelah's voice on the other line. "Hey, Hon."

"Is something going on with the girls?" Donavan comes forward.

Jack holds up a hand and walks a short distance away. When he walks back to where Donavan is bending over the body in the driveway, he motions Donavan away from the deputies standing nearby.

"What's up?"

"Seelah said she was able to zero in on the one who called in on the murdered girl. The man is going to be living here in the cottage where Quigly's place used to be. Guess he will be doing the same thing as Quigly was doin'."

"So this means the Hindel broad is not wasting any time in getting set up here. Did Seelah say what this man's name is?"

"No, just that he's fairly young, in his mid-forties, and big. And that he is very handsome. Maybe Miss Hindel is keeping him on hand to do more than tend the grounds and house."

"She's quite the looker herself. Which reminds me, when you first saw her, you looked as though you'd seen her somewhere before. Have you?"

"Have I what?"

"Seen her somewhere before. Aren't you feeling well? You're not acting like you know what the hell's going on."

"When I saw her, I was blown away by how much she looks like Jillianna Romanitti."

"Hmm, I didn't notice. But then it's been a while since I've seen Jillianna Romanitti."

"Wish I could say the same."

"What do you think is going on with the dreams? Do you find her all that attractive that you want to have dreams of her? I mean, she is one hell of a good-looking woman. I do remember that, but I can see that you are happily married to Seelah."

"There's somethin' strange about these dreams, Donavan. It's almost like I have no choice. But then, we know you sure as hell can't dream about someone every night unless you want to."

"Bullshit, you can't. Remember when I was having those sick dreams about having sex with Chandra, and she was all burned and ugly? It was Seelah who figured out that I was being sent those dreams."

"Yeah, now that you mention it, I do recall that," Jack comes forward. "Aw shit, you don't think this is the work of Jillianna Romanitti, do you?"

"I don't know, but it could be. You remember when she put you in that hypnotic trance and told you that you were her lover in a past life."

"She also claimed we had a kid together, too. A little girl that she had to let go of in order to save the kid's life."

"I know you won't be agreeable to what I am about to suggest, but I think you should talk with Seelah about this. She sure helped me when I was having my dream problems."

"I don't know, you could be right. She was ready to do battle this morning, I know that."

"One thing I have learned in all my years of being married to Barb is don't shut them out. If you have a problem, then share it. Turn the situation around. What if it were Seelah having sex dreams about a handsome man? Wouldn't you be a little up in arms"

"I wish you wouldn't refer to them as sex dreams, Donavan. I already feel bad enough."

"Okay, I guess we've said about all we can about this, so we need to get the coroner out here so we can get the body removed."

"I'll call him."

"Brewster," Donavan turned to the deputy, "Detective Olivier' is going to call the coroner, so you need to get the entire property taped off to show this estate is a crime scene. I hate to tell you this, but you and about eight other deputies are going to be guarding this place to make sure no one else comes on the property. I'll call for some deputies to stay here until you and the others can have dinner and let your families know you are going to be pulling an all-nighter."

"I don't mind telling you, I'm not looking forward to being out here overnight. This damn place gives me the creeps."

"You and everyone else who has ever had anything to do with the place. One thing to always remember when you are on this estate. Always keep your piece unholstered and ready. Things have a way of happening fast here."

"I want to get the rest of the house checked out, and after that, let's go on down and check out the cottage. I'm sure he ain't here yet, but you never know. Could be his vehicle's in the garage."

Finding nothing of importance in the mansion, they walked down to the cottage. After looking in the garage to find no vehicle, they tried all the doors to find them locked.

"We can bet he's gonna be pissed when he finds out he won't be enjoyin' the sweet life of livin' on the Hindel Estate just yet."

"We better leave a note on the cottage door letting him know he can't stay. And I want that gate kept open for the deputies to be able to leave if they need to get the hell out of here."

"Looks like we got company, partner," Jack said as a van drove through the gate."

"That'll be Perkins. I left the gate open until he gets here to do his thing and leave."

Jack stepped into the lane leading up to the mansion as Perkins drives slowly towards him.

"Don't tell me the shit is starting all over again out here." Perkins leans his head out the window of the van.

"Fraid so. Her throat's been ripped out just like the rest down through the years, and from all the blood caked to her legs, it's a sure bet she's been sexually assaulted."

"Sounds like the same M.O. as before. How did you find out about the murder?"

"A man called it in. We're thinkin' it's probably the man who's gonna be the grounds keeper here."

"Is he in the cottage now? If so, I'd like to ask him in what position she was in when he found her."

"No, he must have called in about the murder then left."

Donavan walks over to the van. How's it going, Perkins?" Donavan holds out a hand.

"Hays. Looks like we're back five or six years ago."

"Yeah, looks that way. One thing I'd like you to do is have a check for human saliva done on her. This will give us an idea if we're dealing with Rougarous again."

"Few years back, I recall telling you, you were nuts, but that was before I found the human saliva in the bodies that started popping up."

"Don't feel bad. It took me a while to come to grips with all we were dealing with, too."

"So tell me, who moved into this pile of shit this time?"

"Glad you're already seated. A woman has the estate now.

A woman by the name of Regina Hindel."

CHAPTER 6

Rayford Seals throws the bags of lawn fertilizer in the back of his truck then turns to go back inside the store.

"Rayford, wait a moment. I need to talk with you," Regina calls out to him.

Rayford smiles as he spies her sitting in her small, teal blue Jaguar convertible with the top down. "Guess you heard about the murder out at your place. I found the body when I came up to leave a note on your door earlier."

"Yes, two detectives and their deputies were already there. They told me that since the estate is now a crime scene, I have to stay somewhere else until they are finished with their investigation. I am sure this will apply to you, too."

"That's great. All my clothes and personal items are already in the cottage." He looked down at the tank top and jeans he was wearing. "I was ready to change these boots for a comfortable pair of tennis shoes an hour ago. I doubt they would allow me on the estate long enough to get them. Son of a bitch! I can't even get cleaned up if I am gonna put on the same damn clothes."

"We can find a store, and you can get what personal items

and clothes you need for now. I can write you a check and then take it out of your pay later." She smiles over at him.

Rayford did not return her smile. "I don't see as how this should be considered a loan since what happens on the estate is your problem, not mine. I'm employed to take care of the grounds, not be held up for anything that's not my fault."

"Please, Rayford, don't be difficult. I will pay for your room at the same hotel where I will be staying. You can put your mind at ease and let me take care of everything."

"Alright, I guess that'll work. And, as I said, since what happens on the estate is your problem, my being unable to do my job had better not come out of my pay."

"Your whining is starting to give me a headache. Follow me over to the hotel where we will both be staying. I need to get out of this sun."

"Well, how the hell is this going to work? I just bought all this fertilizer. Now anyone can come and steal it out of the back of my truck."

"Oh, for Pete's sake." Regina gets out of her car and slams the door. "Give me your receipt, and come back in the store with me."

"I don't know why you're gettin' pissed off at me. It'll be your loss if the stuff gets stolen."

Regina snatches the receipt from his hand and walks into the store.

"Hello, I need you to do a favor for me." She shows the man behind the counter her best smile.

"Of course, Miss, I will be glad to help you." The man looked her up and down, enjoying the sight of the beautiful young woman standing before him.

"My grounds keeper just purchased some items for my

lawn, and as something has come up, keeping me from returning to my estate, I am in need of leaving what he purchased here in your store for a few days. I would appreciate your helping me so very much." Regina moved closer to the counter to allow the man who was staring at her with open lust to enjoy the sight of her even more.

"Oh, of course, we can keep everything right here for you, just as long as you need. We pride ourselves on putting our customers first. I certainly hope you are going to be a regular here. Nothin' could please me more."

"You are such a kind man and such a handsome man, too. I will be sure to come in with an order at least once a month, to be sure."

"I'll just start carryin' everything back in the store."

"Rayford, don't just stand there. Give this nice man a hand with carrying all this back in. In the meantime, I will be over at the hotel getting you checked in. When you're through here, come to the hotel."

With a little wave, she walked back to her car, making sure her slim hips wiggle as she moves away.

"That's gotta be one of the best lookin' women I've ever had the pleasure of restin' my eyes on."

"Yeah, she's a looker, all right. Trouble is, she knows it." Rayford stacked another bag of fertilizer in the wheel barrel.

Rayford and the man in the store moved all the fertilizer inside the store until the back of the truck was finally empty.

"Hope to hell none of those sacks were ripped. I for damn sure don't need my truck smellin' like shit."

"Alright, I'll need to have you sign a note here so when you come back to get your fertilizer, you won't have a problem if I'm not here."

"No, that's fine." Rayford scribbled his name on the paper the man pushed over to him. "If all the people are as nice as you, I think I'm gonna enjoy livin' in this place. So what's your name? My name's Rayford Seals. It's a pleasure meetin' you."

"Bud Rawlins, Seals." Bud held out his hand. "So, I heard your boss lady say she has an estate. Not too many of them around. The two of you must be new to the area since I sure would have recalled seein' her if you weren't.

"Her name's Regina Hindel. She just took possession of the Hindel Mansion."

Bud steps away, and turning his back on the man he has been having a friendly conversation with, walks back behind the counter.

"Is somethin' wrong? You seem upset 'bout somethin'." Rayford comes forward.

By now, other people in the store are coming closer to hear what is being said.

"You said the woman who just walked out of here is named Regina Hindel, that she's just taken possession of the Hindel Mansion, and you ask me if something is wrong?"

Loud moans and whispers filter out from the onlookers standing nearby.

"Yeah, Regina Hindel, so? I know she probably ain't well-known here, but she sure as hell is known in New Orleans. The Hindels are old money, and the name is very well known in the city."

"You can believe me when I say the name Hindel is a very well-known name in Saint Anthony Parish. Well known, but for sure not well-liked. Especially by my family."

"Just what are you inferrin' here, and why is everyone standin' 'round starin' at me like I have the plague or somethin'?"

"The last thing this parish needs is for the old Hindel Mansion to fill up again with evil trash!"

"What the hell do you mean, evil trash? I just told you, Regina Hindel and her family are old money from New Orleans. I don't know what all of you have heard, but whatever it is, you best forget it. Regina and I aim to live in this parish, and there ain't a goddamn thing you or anyone else can do about it."

"Is there a problem here, Bud?" A young deputy steps up to the counter."

"Nothin' I can't handle, son. This man works for Regina Hindel, who just moved into the old Hindel Mansion. I was lettin' him know, folks around the parish ain't partial to anyone with the name Hindel."

The deputy puts a hand on the butt of his gun, unsnaps the holster. "Is this going to be a problem, Mister..?"

"Seals. Rayford Seals."

"Things around the parish have been pretty quiet since Lawrence Hindel, and the rest of the Hindels don't live here anymore. Those of us who live here would like to keep it that way."

"I don't have any idea why the people here are up in arms over anyone with the name of Hindel movin' back in the area, but we ain't trouble makers. So, I guess you can rest assured the parish will stay safe even with a Hindel livin' in your midst." Rayford snickers, looking around at the people still standing near the counter.

"This ain't a joke, Mister Seals. You might want to keep a low profile until the folks in the parish know they can remain safe. Also, do you have a concealed weapons permit?

Rayford pulled out his wallet, removing his driver's license and his permit to hand over to the deputy.

"Alright. You would be smart to keep your firearm loaded and on your person at all times." He handed the IDs back to Rayford, and with a brief nod to the man behind the counter, he turns and walks out the door of the store.

"Rayford, you need to come outside right now," Regina calls out to him as she eyes him through the open door of the store.

With a last glance at the people still milling around, gazing at him, he stomps outside.

"These people are all nuts. They seem to think the name Hindel is something to be afraid of."

"I know. I just found out the same thing. We can't get rooms in the hotel. At first, when I checked in, everything was fine, and then the owner of the hotel came to my room and told me to get out that they do not rent rooms to murderers. Me! Regina Hindel being treated like white trash!"

"So what the hell do you suggest we do now? We can't go to the estate, and we can't get a room. We can probably get a room in a cheaper motel out on the highway. Let's try that."

"I will not stay in a filthy motel where hookers and pimps take their customers like I am a poor lowlife. I can't believe I am being treated this way." She began to cry.

"Okay," he swung around, "what the hell do you suggest we do?"

"I'll tell you what we're going to do. Since it is the fault of the police that we are in this mess, it is their place to get us out of the mess!"

"I'll ride with you." He walked around the car and started to get in.

"No," she screeched. "I do not want you in my car and near me. You have been stacking fertilizer. I don't want the smell on my car seats."

"Oh, for Christ's sake! Woman, you're startin' to get on my nerves with your better than everyone else shit!"

"I don't know why I put up with your rough ways."

"You put up with my rough ways because I am the only one who does not bend down and kiss your ass, although I would in a heartbeat if you'd just say the word."

Without a word, she turned the key and roared off down the street quickly, followed by an irate Rayford Seals.

CHAPTER 7

Standing on the patio, Donavan squeezes his twist of lime into the glass filled with Scotch and water before taking a small sip. He smiles as he walks over to sit down on one of the lawn chairs pulled up to a round patio table.

"God knows I needed this after what we just ran into earlier."

Jack takes the chair next to Donavan. "It's nice to enjoy a drink because you want to instead of because you have to." He pours a bottle of beer into a frosty mug of tomato juice.

Donavan glances over at him, then nods. "Yeah, I'm sure it is."

Barbara bends down, placing a loud kiss atop Donavan's head. "I love you, Donavan and I know it had to be a shock to the two of you finding out that another Hindel is moving into the mansion."

Donavan reaches up and pulls her head down to plant a kiss on her full mouth. "Shock is an understatement. But, I have to admit, since a body has been found on the estate, I'm not surprised a Hindel is most likely involved."

"What does this new Hindel look like?"

"She doesn't look like anything out of the ordinary. Just another Hindel to make our lives miserable," Jack speaks up.

"The woman moving into the Hindel Mansion is anything but ordinary. To tell the truth, she is beautiful." Seelah stood beside Jack's chair.

"She has nothing on my beautiful woman." Jack pulls Seelah into his lap. "My woman is steak and potatoes. The Hindel woman is cotton candy. Good for a little while, but no one wants to have cotton candy every day."

Seelah burst out laughing. "I have never had anyone describe me as a steak and potato woman, Jack."

"You're not only steak and potatoes, Baby. You're a hot fudge Sundae with a cherry on top."

Donavan laughs, glad to see Jack and Seelah getting along, then reaches for his cell phone as it begins to ring.

"Probably one of the deputies we left to guard the crime scene checking in." He turns and picks up his phone. "Lieutenant Hays here."

Jack glances over at Donavan, noting the angry scowl coming across his face.

"We'll be there in a few minutes." He clicks off his phone. "What's up?"

"Seems, when people in the parish heard the name Hindel they got up in arms. The Hindel woman and her groundskeeper are having a hard time getting a room. She seems to think this is our problem, and she wants the problem righted right now. This, according to dispatch. I told him we'd be there to take care of things."

"She sounds like a real handful," Barbara laughed as she walks over to the portable bar.

"She's a spoiled brat. She thinks anything she wants or anything she says is the way it is."

"Guess it's time to go to work. I knew this day was going too good."

"Donny and I are going to hang out here with Barb and Jenny. We can continue our fun day when the two of you get back."

"I don't mind telling you. This pisses me off. I like spending time with family. We see enough of the station during the week. And, it goes without saying that now that we have a murder on our hands, the brass is going to want it solved as fast as possible."

"We should tell the brass if they want the murders to stop in the parish, then they should post a sign beside the one welcoming newcomers to Saint Anthony Parish, saying NO HINDELS ALLOWED."

"Yeah, don't I wish?"

***

"How much longer are we going to have to stay here? I am tired, and I would like to go and have dinner and relax," Regina tells the man behind the desk.

"I already told you, Miss, Lieutenant Hays and Detective Olivier' are on their way here to talk to you. You need to have a seat and wait."

"Oh, I cannot stand the ineptness of people."

"Oh, for Christ's sake, Regina. The man is doing the best he can. Come over here and sit down on the bench."

"Don't you dare speak to me in that commanding tone. I am your employer. I am the one in command of this situation, not some $10.00 an hour cop!" Regina whirls on him.

Rayford grabs hold of her arm to yank her further down the hall. "Now you listen to me, goddamn it! Your last name is the reason we are being treated like shit in this parish, so you need to cool your heels and shut the fuck up! These cops can throw our asses behind bars for no reason, and they would love to do just that! I didn't sign on to spend time in jail! So, unless you want to be in this mess alone, I suggest you quit actin' like a bitch, and set down!"

"Miss Hindel, I understand you are having a hard time getting motel accommodations." Donavan walks up to the two people glaring at one another.

"Yes, we are, and it is all your fault."

"How is it my fault?" Donavan is trying to remain calm.

"You refuse to allow me to stay in my house. And now, I am being refused a room."

"I already explained to you that the estate is a crime scene because a female was found murdered on the property. And too, you have yet to show proof that you have a legal right to be on the Hindel Estate."

"How do you propose I prove my right to be in my house?"

"First off, you need to calm down. We are all adults here, so let's act like it. We can all go and talk in my office, and you can place a call to your attorney."

"Well, where is your office? I am not going to stand here all day while you play detective games!"

Jack pulls Rayford off to the side. "How the hell did you come to get hooked up with this broad? She might be easy on the eyes, but for Christ's sake, if she ain't puttin' out, you need to hit the road cause I'll tell ya, buddy, anyone with the name of Hindel is nothin' but trouble in this parish."

"You don't have any reason to talk 'bout her like this. You don't even know her."

"No, you're right, I don't, but I've sure as hell've known

plenty of her kin."

"Have a seat, Miss Hindel." Donavan motions to a chair near his desk.

"Jack, if you and Mr. Seals would like to come in and shut the door, we can get on to solving the problems of the day."

Regina sits down in the chair, and unzipping her purse, she pulls a small cell phone into view. She quickly touches some numbers, then waits. "This is Miss Hindel calling to speak with Mr. Clayton. Of course, it is important! Otherwise, I would not be bothering to call. I don't care if he is in a meeting with another client. I am the client he needs to be concerned about."

"I gotta tell ya," Jack leans forward, "she might be goodlookin', but there ain't no pussy worth puttin' up with this much bullshit!"

Donavan nods, settling himself back in his chair to wait.

"I need you to speak to a cop who doesn't believe I am now the legal owner of the Hindel Mansion."

Donavan holds out his hand for her phone. "This is Lieutenant Donavan Hays of the Saint Anthony Parish Sheriff's Department, Mr. Clayton. You will need to call my office after we hang up. I have one of your clients, a Miss Regina Hindel, in my office claiming to be the owner of an estate here in the parish. Please call area code 504-555-0926. Thank you, Mr. Clayton." Donavan hands the phone back to an angry Regina Hindel.

"You had my attorney on the phone. Why didn't you simply conduct your business while you were speaking with him? All you are doing is wasting time."

"While you are living here in the parish, you will do things the way I see fit, Miss Hindel. You are not in New Orleans now." Donavan reaches out as his phone begins to ring.

"Is he always this hard on newcomers to the parish, or

is he only this way with people whose last name is, Hindel?" Rayford speaks up, his tone angry.

Jack grins. "I don't get it. You said you lived in New Orleans and are familiar with the Hindel name. If this is so, then how the hell did you miss knowin' everything the Hindels are into?"

"Case you ain't noticed, Regina Hindel and me do not run in the same circles. She's Beluga Caviar and Dom Perigon. I'm brats and Corona beer."

"Whether you party together or not, you've had to of heard `bout all the killin's the Hindel family has had a hand in, or I should say a claw in. Tell ya what, how `bout you and me take a walk outside and have a smoke?"

"Sounds good. You're startin' to pique my interest in this Hindel shit, especially since a woman was found on the estate with her throat ripped out."

"Donavan, I think you can handle this without me. Seals and me are gonna take a little stroll outside for a smoke."

"Yeah, go ahead. Miss Hindel and I can get better acquainted while you're gone."

"We won't be long."

"Alright, Miss Hindel, your attorney has verified that yes, you are now the legal owner of the Hindel estate. Now what we need to talk about is how much do you know about the Hindel Family?"

***

"Let's go set on this bench over here, Seals." Jack walks them across the lawn to a bench with a large ashtray cemented in the front.

"Okay, now what the hell is all this `bout the Hindels you feel I should already know?"

Jack shakes a cigarette from the package then reaches for his lighter. "Seals, have you ever heard of a creature called a Rougarou?"

"Ain't that like a werewolf or something? What the hell does a werewolf have to do with what we're talkin' 'bout?"

"Are you ready for the truth?" Jack eyes the other man through a haze of blue smoke.

"Would you get to the fuckin' point here, detective? I'm ready for a cold beer and somethin' to eat."

"A Rougarou is a creature covered with short black hair and claw-like hands and has the face of a human."

"Okay, and what the hell does this have to do with Regina Hindel?"

"For many years, this parish was infested with Rougarous. This is why the two of you are gettin' shunned in the parish. And the man who you bought your fertilizer from, a Mr. Rawlins?"

"Yeah, that was his name."

"His brother and sister-in-law and their children lived in the Hindel Mansion at one time. Their daughter disappeared, never to be found, and then, later on, the rest of the family was murdered.

"And because this took place in the Hindel Mansion, you're sayin' this is the fault of the owner at the time? Was it proven that the owner was the killer?"

"At the time of the murders, Jonathan Hindel was said to be in England."

"But you don't agree, right?"

"No, I don't. Lawrence Hindel, the young man thought to be Jonathan's son, was put on trial for the murders."

"Of course, the killer had to be a Hindel. So, did Lawrence get hung out for the crimes?"

"No, he was found not guilty by reason of insanity. He spent a few years in a mental institution and then was pronounced cured, and then released."

"Do you believe Lawrence was guilty?" Rayford peered over at him.

"No, I don't. I did at first, but from all the things that happened later, it was obvious Lawrence was not the guilty party. He was just the one who took the fall for the murders."

"There, you see, you can't blame the Hindels for all that happens in the mansion. And speakin' of Hindels, I best go check on the Hindel who will be signin' my paychecks."

"You didn't ask who was finally found guilty of the murders." Jack stubs out his cigarette in the ashtray.

Seals stops, and turns around. "Are you gonna tell me, or keep it to yourself?"

"Jonathan Hindel was the killer."

"Of course. Jonathan Hindel had to be the killer since his name was Hindel, right?"

"No, Jonathan Hindel was not the one found to be the killer because his last name was Hindel. Jonathan Hindel was found to be the killer because he was a Rougarou."

"That does it. I'm gonna go get Regina and get the both of us the hell outta here." Seals stomps off towards the door to the station.

Jack falls in beside him. "Believe it or not, I know just how you feel. It took me a while to believe all this shit, too."

"As much as I need the money, I can't be a part of believin' there are monsters lurkin' 'round killin' people."

"If you and the Hindel woman are gonna be livin' here in the parish, then you need to know what the hell is goin' on."

"Look, you might be a cop and able to throw my ass in jail,

but I'm warnin' you right goddamn now if you go in that room and frighten Regina with all your monster bullshit, I will kick the livin' shit outta you."

"You can try. I won't throw you in jail for what you see as protectin' your employer, but you both need to know what evil lives in this parish.

Rayford's hand was already on the door knob when an angry Regina Hindel comes flying through the door, all but knocking Rayford off his feet.

"You need to get me the hell out of here right now. This place is filled with lunatics."

"Miss Hindel, I will have one of my deputies escort you to a motel out on the highway where the two of you can get rooms for a few days until the investigation is completed." Donavan follows her outside.

Regina whirls to face him, her eyes flashing the heated anger she is feeling. "I already told you, we are not staying in a crab-infested motel room where hookers ply their trade. God only knows what we could catch."

"Then the only thing you can do is sleep in your vehicles since you can't go to your estate, and no one here will rent you a room."

"Looks to me like you're between sweat and shit, Miss Hindel," Jack tells her, not bothering to wipe the wide grin from his face.

"Yes, you're right. We will just stay in Rayford's truck." She motions Rayford to follow her.

Donavan walks over to his jeep and, unlocking the door, reaches in for his handheld radio. "This is Lieutenant Hays. Be on the lookout for a man and a woman who will be coming onto the property. You will arrest them and bring them into the station in cuffs."

CHAPTER 8

Brewster clicks off his handheld radio and walks back up onto the front porch.

"Guess we got company on the way."

Deputy John Hendrickson takes a chair beside him. "I hope the company you're referring to is more cops. This goddamn place makes me sick to my stomach, and we can never have too many guns."

Brewster's hand shot out, silencing him.

"What the hell! Did you see something?" Hendrickson whispers.

"Yeah." He pulls his radio into position. "This is Brewster. All deputies are to come to the front of the house. Now! I think we got company."

"Maybe it's the couple Hays just called in about."

"No," he whispers, leaning in close. "Look straight out towards the swamp and tell me what you see."

With the full moon overhead, they could both see two creatures standing near each other, looking their way.

"Oh my god, they can't be human." He shudders, trying

to keep his fear at a safe distance. "So many stories about this place we all grew up hearing and laughed at, telling ourselves they weren't true. Now we see what everyone has been talking about. And to make matters worse, we got a man and a woman on their way here," Brewster says.

"I think we better let Hays and Olivier' in on what we have."

"Good idea."

"I'm going to call in on the cell. Otherwise, anyone with a scanner can know what we have out here, and before you know what's what, we'll be overcome with looky-loos."

"I hate this fuckin' place," Hendrickson said as they walked to the patrol car to get the cell phone.

"You and me both. If my wife wasn't expecting another kid, I'd look for another job, but the insurance we have through the department is too good to walk away from."

"Beats the hell out of the shit the government's trying to push on people." He grabs his cell off the dashboard. "Hays and Olivier' aren't going to like this."

***

"Alright, we have that handled. So now we can go home and enjoy the rest of the evening with family." Donavan picks up his keys to the jeep off the desk.

"You know we're gonna get a call when the Hindel broad and her fuck buddy show up. We might as well stay here."

"I'm not going to hang around here. They've got orders to bring them in and throw their asses in a cell. I'm going home and enjoy myself with a strong drink and something good on TV."

Jack stands up, then sits back down as the phone on the desk rings.

"Damn, that was quick. I didn't think they'd have enough

time to even get out there." Donavan grabs up the receiver. "Lieutenant Hays," he barks, not quieting the tone of his voice. "Alright, get all the men in the front of the house in one spot. We're on our way."

"What the hell's goin' on now?"

"Brewster spotted two creatures down near the swamp area. He thinks they're Rougarous, and since we've already seen their leavings, I tend to agree with him."

"Son of a bitch! This shit's startin' all over again."

"Call Barb and tell her what's going on and that we may be gone all night. Be a good idea for Seelah and Donny to stay where they are with Barb."

They hastened their steps to the jeep. Within moments they were speeding to the Hindel Mansion.

***

"I don't think we should drive all the way up to the house. They have detectives standing guard."

"Drive all the way to the house. I am not going to be wandering around out here with a killer on the loose."

"Goddamn it, Regina. You're gonna get both our asses in jail for returnin' to a crime scene after we've been warned to stay away."

"You will do as you're told."

Hey, you know what? Fuck you and your job. You ain't worth my doin' jail time over. I'm leavin'. Are you comin' with me, or do you want to get out here and walk to the house?"

Regina stared at him. "You would actually leave me out here alone with no protection?"

"Oh, trust me, you'll have plenty of protection. You'll have about ten or more cops around you.

Regina reaches out and turns off the key, then pulls the set of keys out of the ignition.

"We are both going to go to the house." She turns, getting out of the truck.

"Crazy god damn broad is gonna get us both in trouble." Rayford reaches under his seat and pulls out a flashlight, then opening the door on his side, he slides out of the truck.

They can hear the grunting of gators as they leave the banks to splash back into the water.

Regina grabs Rayford's hand. "Oh my god. What was that?"

"Gators. I hope you ain't scared of snakes cause this place is crawlin' with them, too."

"You're going to have to put up a fence to keep them from coming close to the house."

"That would work for the gators, but there's no way in hell you're gonna keep snakes corralled. They crawl up the trees and hang down. One could be getting ready to curl around your neck right now."

"Stop it. You're trying to frighten me." Her voice is little more than a whisper.

"Quiet!" Rayford tells her, his voice harsh and low.

"Stop it. I will—"

"I said be quiet. I'm not playin'. Something's over there by those trees."

Rayford aimed the beam of his flashlight in the direction he had seen a movement.

"What the fuck? Do you see what I see?

"What are you seeing?" Regina moves over closer. "It's probably the deputies who are guarding the estate."

"Deputies hell! That ain't no god damn deputy!" Rayford clicks the flashlight on high beam and aims it at the trees.

Two grotesque faces turn into the beam of light to stare out at them, making Regina scream.

Rayford grabs her by the arm as they both run for the safety of the truck. "Get in. We need to get the hell outta here. Whatever those things are, they ain't human!"

Rayford starts the truck and backs up until they are back on the lane. They are almost to the gate when a jeep pulls up, blocking their way.

"Get the fuck outta the way!" Rayford's voice is harsh as he yells out the window.

Donavan and Jack walk up to the truck with their guns drawn.

"You two were told you could not come back here until our investigation is finished. Now, it looks like you're going to be spending the night in our jail."

"We don't care where we spend the night as long as it isn't here. Something is out there." Regina shivers.

"Now you know what the hell we've been trying to tell you."

"My guess would be, some of your kin folk' has come callin', Miss Hindel. Looks like you ain't too hospitable."

"God damn it!" Rayford throws open his door and slides out of the truck. "Either you're gonna leave her the hell alone, or you're gonna get your ass kicked."

Donavan steps between the two. "Alright, we don't need any fighting. We have enough problems with what's out there."

"Then tell him to shut his mouth."

"You need to show a little respect for the law, Slick. You're not supposed to be here in the first place."

"I have respect for the law, god damn it! But I sure as hell will not stand here while you throw slurs at Miss Hindel."

"Jack, you need to let me handle this. You're both too hot-headed," Donavan warns him

"I think I have made a big mistake coming to live in this parish. You all act as though you were brought up by ghetto trash."

At the same time Jack flips Seals around and snaps the cuffs into place, Donavan does the same with Regina.

"Playtime is over." Donavan motioned one of the two deputies standing nearby to come forward. "Take these two to the station and book them. The reason will be hindering a police investigation and coming back to a crime scene after being told to stay away."

"You are not serious! You will remove these handcuffs now! I am Regina Hindel. I will not be treated this way!"

At that moment, a high-pitched howl splits the silence, making all who hear it freeze in place.

"Comin' from the swamp," Jack whispers. "We need to check out the house again. There could be another secret panel into a cave just like before."

"Oh my god. What was that?"

"Still want to stay here now, Miss Hindel?" Donavan reaches behind her to remove the cuffs.

"What? That was just a large animal. Rayford, don't you think that is what it was, just a large animal?" Seeing the look of fear on Rayford's face as he looks around the area, she nods. "Alright then, yes, please get me out of here."

"I'll release both of you, but only if you promise not to return to the estate until we tell you it is alright to do so. Also, I'll have one of my deputies get you a room at one of the better motels for a few days."

"Thank you, detective. I would appreciate it. However, I

would rather stay at a nice hotel. They have room service. I'm sure you understand. And too, we will need two rooms. Rayford is only my hired man."

Donavan glances at her briefly before turning to one of his deputies. "Hendrickson, lead them to the SHAY Hotel, and tell the man at the desk I said it will be alright to rent them a room for a few days."

"Yes, sir, Lieutenant Hays."

"The Shay Hotel is the best we have to offer. I'm sure you'll both be happy there." He walks over to the jeep and grabs his handheld off the seat.

"Dispatch, this is Lieutenant Hays. I need at least four cars with four deputies in each. They will be securing the Hindel Estate until further notice. Also, we're going to need K9s first thing in the morning."

"I feel sorry for who's ever on dispatch, having to relay that message." Jack laughs outright.

"You and me both."

"I have to tell you, I'm starting to feel a little sorry for Regina Hindel."

"Oh yeah, my heart pumps gilded piss for her, too. She could buy and sell both of us. She should have checked out what she was gettin' herself into before she jumped."

"If she had no way of knowing what owning the Hindel Mansion would entail, then she is not to blame."

Another high-pitched howl splits the air.

"That howl came from the house this time. Son of a bitch, they're inside the mansion."

They drive through the gate just as it closes, stopping the cars behind them. "Someone closed the fuckin' gate," Jack yells, speeding towards the front of the mansion.

Without warning, they see a dark shadow move in front of the window in the kitchen where the control panel for the gate is.

With guns drawn, they run through the door. "Let me get the gate opened, then we will have enough backup to be with us when we wait for daylight. I would rather check this place out in the light of day when you can see what you're dealing with."

The screeching of vehicles out front draws their attention.

"The K9s should have no problem trackin' that shadow lookin' son of a bitch. Bet you anything, he leads us down to the basement."

"Don't be too sure. Lawrence knew we were onto the secret panel leading to the basement and up from the lake."

"So you're sayin' he had a different secret panel and room built into this dump?"

"I wouldn't doubt it."

"Since we're going to wait out the night, you better call the girls and let them know that there will be no sleep for us tonight.

CHAPTER 9

Jillianna finishes her glass of wine, setting the empty glass on the small table beside her bed. Getting to her feet, she drops the sheer robe she is wearing to the floor.

"Tonight, there will be no holding back," she whispers into the quiet. "Tonight, you will be my lover, Karleto, just as you were all those years ago."

After rolling the covers to the bottom of the bed, she takes her place in the middle, breathing deeply to relax her mind.

Soon she feels her spirit lift from her body. She can feel the cool night air caress her skin. She soars through the air until finally, she sees the small house below. Within moments, Jillianna is in the Olivier' bedroom, only to find the room empty. Unwilling to be deterred, she moves out further into the house.

"Where are you? It is late. You should be home in bed."

She can feel the building anger creep over her as the minutes are ticked off on the small clock sitting on the bedside table, and still, there is no sign of anyone in the Olivier' house.

Jillianna waits throughout the long night only to find herself still alone when the early morning sun shines through the windows of the empty house.

"You will not be able to keep me away, Karleto. You belong to me, and soon you will know this."

***

Donavan and Jack sit down on the front porch of the mansion while they wait for the deputies with the K9s to show up.

"Strange there could be this much beauty to be found in such a place of evil." Donavan looks around at the well-manicured lawn and the garden of flowers in full bloom. "Rather like having a beautiful rose dropped into a nest of vipers."

"Wonder who's been keepin' up the grounds? Been a while since Lawrence and his bitch were here to tend to things."

"Good question. Now you have me wondering. I doubt anyone in the parish would be stupid enough to come out here to work."

"Unless they have nothin' to fear."

"Let's just leave it at that. We haven't had any sleep, and the thought of the parish bein' overrun with Hindels has me pissed off to the point of buyin' up every stick of dynamite out there and blowin' this fuckin' place off its foundation. Again.

"The K9s are here. Now we can find out what is what. That shadow didn't disappear into thin air."

"Glad you could finally make it. We need to check this shack out from top to bottom. We saw a shadow in the kitchen during the night." Donavan says.

"Come on, boy, let's go solve the mystery of the hiding Rougarous," the deputy said, leading his dog into the house.

"How will he react when he finds where a Rougarou went into a secret room?" Donavan follows behind the deputy.

"He'll lie down in front of the room, just as he is doing

now." The deputy smiled, patting his dog on the head.

"All right, we've found the room. Now the problem is how the hell do we get into the sonofabitch?"

Jack walks across the thick carpet and up to the wall the K9 has picked up on, as being where someone or something is hidden. Jack taps on the wall, then listens to see if the sounds coming back to him indicate a secret room has been added.

Donavan walks over to him. "There has to be a hidden devise just as there was to open the wall in the basement in the old mansion."

"Yeah, but where the hell is it? If it was up to me, I'd take an ax and open this up and let loose every shell on whatever crawls out."

"I feel the same, but it wouldn't be your ass responsible for the cost of the damage. It would be mine."

"Lieutenant Hays, the second crew just arrived," Deputy Hendrickson told him. "What do you want me to tell them?"

"That's all right, Deputy. I'll come out and tell them where they need to be stationed. You and last night's crew can head for home to get some rest. Good chance you will all be back here tonight for another all-nighter," Donald delivered, turning away as his phone begins to ring. "Lieutenant Hays."

"Yeah, Hays, Perkins here. Thought I'd let you know I have the results of your autopsy."

"Damn, that was fast. Usually, it takes you at least a few weeks to get back to us."

"I put a rush on the tests. I knew you'd be anxious to hear what we found."

"You sure have a different tone and opinion on how things need to get done now that you know another Hindel is living in the mansion. A lot different than a few years ago."

"Alright, you don't need to rub it in. A few years ago, I was no more in the know than the rest of the parish."

"So, what did you find? I bet this time, you checked for human saliva."

Donavan could hear Perkins cuss under his breath.

"Goddamn it, Hays, do you want to hear the results or not? I got things I need to get to."

"I'm waiting."

"The results show there was an abundance of human saliva mixed in with animal fur in the blood found on the body."

"Then I guess we can assume the killer is a Rougarou, right?"

"I don't think I can go that far, but whatever it is, I have to admit I have never run across it. "I don't feed into the theory of the Rougarou being a werewolf. But, again, whatever it is, it sure as hell is not human. Anyway, I need to get back to work, so that's all I have for you."

"Thanks, Perkins. I appreciate you getting on the results right away

"What did Perkins have to offer? Anything of importance or was he just callin' to let you know it will be a few weeks before he has anything to offer?"

"Believe it or not, he already has the test results finished, and he admitted to finding human saliva and animal fur in the blood on the body."

Shaking his head, Jack walks away.

"All right, I am sure by now you all know what is coming down in the parish again. Another murder on the Hindel Estate. And from the autopsy findings, human saliva and animal fur were found on the victim."

Jack stands back, watching the different expressions

crossing the deputies' faces. At first, the most apparent look to come forth was one of fear, but as they stood there, another, more dominant, expression took over. A look of all-out killing anger.

"I see you all feel the same as Lieutenant Hays and me. You want to catch these sons of bitches, and get rid of them once and for all."

One of the deputies speaks up. He was younger than the others, but the anger covering his handsome face is no less than that of the more seasoned officers. "Why can't this place be blown to hell just like the last mansion was?"

Donavan glanced at his nameplate. "I wish it were this simple, Deputy Andrew Tapio, because nothing could please me any more than to do just that. Again. Anyway, the estate has a new owner. Her name is Regina Hindel. She and the man she has hired on to take care of the grounds are not allowed on the estate until we have finished our investigation."

"In other words, as much as I hate to say this, we are starting all over with the mess we thought we were through with five years ago," Jack entered into the conversation.

"This can't be true." Deputy Tapio looks around at the other deputies. "My wife and I were so afraid to have kids here that we even talked about moving out of the parish. But when Lawrence Hindel was killed, and it was thought that all the Hindels were dead, we decided it was alright to start a family. Now we have two little boys, and you're standing here telling me it's all happening again?"

"I'm afraid so," Donavan said. "I think the best thing all of you can do if you have a wife is to get her a .38 and teach her how to use it."

"I thought a Rougarou couldn't be killed with a regular bullet."

"The jury of logic is still out on that one, Deputy Tapio. Before, we were going on the theory of the Rougarou being like the werewolf, that it can only be killed with a silver bullet. This is what books and movies had to offer. Now we know that the Rougarou is not a make-believe monster. The Rougarou is real.

"In any case, even if it doesn't kill the son of a bitch it will slow it down," Jack told them.

"We need to get at least three of you started on looking in the living room for a device to open a hidden panel. It won't be very big, maybe only a button that, when pushed it will open a wall," Donavan said.

"Alright, you, you, and you," Jack points to three deputies, "come with us, and the rest of you go in pairs to secure the grounds.

Donavan and Jack, followed by the three deputies, walk into the mansion and over to a bare wall.

"You'd think, so as not to call attention to a wall that hides a secret room, they would at least hang a picture or two on the damn thing. All the rest of the walls are decorated."

"We're talkin' 'bout Hindels, and how they think, or for that matter, don't think," Jack said.

"Be my guess, the button would be behind a picture hung on the wall. Remember, Lawrence was not the sharpest of thinkers."

"You're right, Detective Olivier'. It's right here," Tapio says as he lays a picture down on a nearby end table.

Donavan walks over to the button. "I want all of you to unholster your weapons and be ready for anything that might come flying out of this room. If anything does come flying out of this room, I want each and every one of you to empty your weapons into what will be a threat to our lives."

With that said, Donavan pushes the button, then stands ready with his gun aimed at the wall.

As the wall swings open, two men run out of the room only to be met with gunfire.

Screams split the silence as the men fall, bleeding on the floor of the living room.

"I want the three of you to go outside. Lieutenant Hays and I can handle this," Jack tells the deputies.

As the door closes behind the departing deputies, Donavan walks over to stand beside Jack. "Jack, I know what you have in mind."

"You're damn right you know what I have in mind. I hope you're not gonna try'n talk me out of it." Jack kicked each man over on his stomach and, reaching down, pulls a wallet out of his back pocket before kicking the man back over onto his back.

"Since I can't let you do this alone, I might as well get in on the fun."

Sounds of rapid gunfire exploding in the room brought all three deputies running back into the house. "They tried to attack. We had no choice but to waste'm," Jack glanced over at the staring deputies.

"I don't think we have to worry about them going after another young girl in the parish."

"No, I'd say it's a pretty safe bet they're done for. Can't very well turn into a flesh-eatin' Rougarou when the sun goes down with their heads shot off." Jack laughs openly.

"Let's see who they are." Donavan flips open one of the wallets. "This says he was Renaldo P. Hindel. Guess the P stands for prick. Check the other wallet, Jack.

"What the hell?" Jack looked over at Donavan. "Guess the Hindels ain't the only ones who go in for bein' Rougarous."

"Nothing strange about that fact. If you remember right, most of the biggies in this parish were Rougarous."

"Yeah, but I think we might know who this piece of shit is related to."

Donavan looked down at the man's ID and drew in his breath. "Andrei Romanitti. Holy shit! This is going to be one for the books."

"Now we get the privilege of letting Jillianna Romanitti know she has a relative she's gonna need to get planted."

CHAPTER 10

Jillianna peeks around the corner of the kitchen as she hears the front doorbell ring. Within moments she hears the sound of Baxter's voice as he ushers the callers inside. Quickly, she stepped back into the kitchen to pour herself a cup of coffee.

"Madam," Baxter says as he walks over to her, "you have visitors. Detective Hays and Detective Olivier' wish to talk with you."

"Thank you, Baxter. I will be right there. In the meantime, you can offer them something to drink."

"Yes'm, Ms. Jillianna." He turns away to go back into the living room.

Jillianna moves to the guest bathroom. Grabbing up a hairbrush, she runs the brush over her long hair. Satisfied with her appearance, she walks from the room.

"What a pleasant surprise," she smiles, her eyes looking only on the face of the man who fills her every waking moment.

Jack glances away, glad when Donavan steps forward with the ID of the man they had just killed in his hand.

"We're here on official business, Miss Romanitti. A woman

was murdered on the Hindel Estate last night, and we found the ID of a man with the last name of Romanitti. Since the name Romanitti is not that common, we thought you would want to know one of your relatives is in need of a proper burial."

Jillianna reaches out, taking the ID from Donavan's outstretched hand. "Although I do not recall this person, as he carries the Romanitti name, I will see to what needs to be done."

"Thank you. We will be going now as I am sure you have more important things to do than visiting with us. I will let you know when you can claim the body for burial." Donavan turns to leave.

Jillianna comes forward. "How did you come to find this man's ID on the Hindel Estate?"

Jack held up a hand as Donavan starts to speak up. "We found the name in his wallet after he and another man came runnin' out of a secret room inside the mansion."

"I don't understand."

"We found a secret room inside the mansion. When we opened it up, two men came running out of the room. Since we are investigating the murder of a young woman found on the estate, we knew our lives could be in danger from the two men running towards us. We shot the sons of bitches then pulled their wallets out of their pockets to see who they were. One was Romanitti, and the other was a Hindel."

"I see. If you felt your lives were threatened, of course, you had no choice."

"I can let the Medical Examiner know that since this man is not a close relative, there will be no reason for you to have to identify the body," Donavan tells her.

"What Detective Hays is saying," he walks over close to her, "is he wants to save you the ordeal of seeing this individual with his head blown off."

"You had to shoot him in the head to stop him?" she whispers.

"No, we didn't have to since he was already dead. We wanted to. See, we wanted to make sure the evil fuck didn't come back again as a Rougarou."

"What makes you think he was a Rougarou?" Jillianna lowers her voice as she moves closer to Jack.

Instinctively, Jack steps back. "We were told by the people who will be living on the estate as soon as our investigation is over that they saw two creatures down near the gate during the night. Their descriptions fit what we know a Rougarou to look like."

Jillianna reaches out, putting one hand on Jack's arm. "Who are the people moving onto the estate?"

"Get your hands off me." Jack's voice is low and filled with anger. "I don't want you anywhere near me."

"Why, Jack?" Jillianna purrs. "Is something wrong?"

"You know goddamn well, there's somethin' wrong. I don't know what kind of voodoo or witch shit you're usin' on me, but it's gonna stop right goddamn now!"

"If you explain what you are talking about, perhaps I can better understand what is going on with you that involves me."

Jillianna stands looking at Jack and tries to quiet the pain racing through her body at his harsh treatment of her.

"Don't give me that poor me look. You're comin' into my dreams every goddamn night in an attempt to make me cheat on my wife." Jack sticks a finger in her face to strengthen his anger! "Are you that hard up that you have to try and seduce a man who has nothin' but loathin' for you?"

"If I remember right, you seemed to enjoy yourself as

much as I did." Jillianna smiles into his face.

"Jack!" Donavan steps forward as Jack's hand draws back. "Even though she did ask for it, she is still a woman, and we are still professionals."

"Let's get the hell outta here, `fore I knock her through the wall."

"Right behind you, partner," Donavan says as they walk out the door.

Jillianna walks over to the large plate window, watching as they get into their vehicle. The tears streaming down her face are left to fall unnoticed.

"Ms. Jillianna, is there anything I can get you to make you feel better?" Baxter asked, gazing at her from across the room and shaking his head at his inability to help her.

"Yes, Baxter, there is something you can do for me," she says as she watches the jeep disappear down the long lane leading from her mansion. "You can order me a friend to make me forget my troubles this night. Make sure he looks as much like Detective Oliver' as possible."

***

"I can't believe you were going to slap the living hell out of her. I saw a side of you I've never known existed and would have bet money that it didn't exist."

"Evil bitch needs to stay outta my life. I went through enough shit with Chandra. I'm not gonna stand still for it again."

Donavan looks away as he recalls the beautiful quadroon Jack had lost his heart to some years back and too, how close he had come to almost losing his life.

"Remember, Chandra turned out to be a good person who had no choice in what she was putting you through. Never know; this Romanitti person could have an ulterior motive for what she is putting you through."

"We already know why she's puttin' moves on me. She believes I'm her lost lover in a past life. Remember? This is what she told me when she put me in that fuckin' trance."

"I still think it would be to your advantage to tell Seelah what is going on. As I said, she helped me. Let her help you, Jack."

"Tell you the truth, I'm afraid to have her anywhere near my family. She's a goddamn vampire, remember? What if she gets angry enough to attack Seelah and Donny?"

"If she comes near Seelah and Donny, she will not live long. You and your family are an extension of my own family. You know this."

"I don't even know how you go 'bout killin' a vampire. The same as you would a Rougarou, I guess."

"Maybe you should start wearing a cross and filling the room with garlic every night."

"This is no time for jokes, Donavan. We're not in a damn horror movie. We're in the real world."

"Talk about your oxymorons. I have never known the real world to include a vampire."

"Yeah, well, this is Saint Anthony Parish where anything from a fuckin' Rougarou to a vampire can live and does!"

At the same time, both men burst out laughing.

CHAPTER 11

The desk clerk at the Shay Hotel laid a room key on the desk in front of the handsome couple checking into the hotel. He shot a brief nod to the departing deputy, who had told him the sheriff's department was okaying their right to stay in the hotel.

"You have made a mistake. We will need two rooms." Her dark eyes look upward as she breathes a deep sigh. "This man is only my hired help."

"Only time will tell how long that will last," Rayford murmured, his dark gaze turning hostile as he looks at her.

"Do you have an eating facility in the hotel? We would like to have dinner before we retire to our rooms." Regina's tone is haughty as she stares over at the man behind the desk.

"Yes, Madam. We have a top of the line restaurant here in the hotel. I am sure you will be pleased with the cuisine we have to offer. Both our chefs come from New Orleans."

"That is a plus." She glanced over at Rayford, who stood, his jaw clenched tight, silently watching her. "In that case, maybe something will finally turn out, and we can have an enjoyable meal."

"Yes, Madam, and if you find you need anything once you go to your rooms, you need only call down to the desk, and we will send someone up to take care of your needs."

"All right, and if I do, please let your staff know I do not like to be kept waiting. Now, where is your restaurant so we can stop wasting time and have dinner?"

"Right through those doors," he told her, nodding off to her left.

"Come along, Rayford." Regina steps in front of him as she moves towards the heavy doors.

"Thank you for being such a professional. I know it isn't an easy thing to do when dealing with her," Rayford said as he leans over the desk.

"You just made my job look a whole lot more desirable," the night clerk tells him, a wide grin covering his face.

"Are you going to stand talking with the help, or are you coming with me?" Regina stands, her hands balled on her slender hips.

Without a word, Rayford walks towards her. "Don't you ever treat me like your hired slave again. If you do, you can take this job and stick it straight up your self-centered ass!"

"What? Would you rather I let him think you're my hired stud?" She glowered at him.

"I'm beginning to think you need a good stud to bend you over and wear your ass out." He grabs her arm and propels her into the very elaborate-looking restaurant.

"Do you have reservations for this evening, and if so, what is the name?" The man standing before a small podium with a large, open book asked.

"Yes, we have reservations." Regina hands him a crisp bill.

He bowed slightly. "Of course, Madam, right this way."

"You have all the answers, don't you, Regina?"

"What do you mean?" She opened the menu.

"I mean, if the rules don't fit, then you simply pull out a little money and make them fit."

"Don't be naïve, Rayford. The rules only apply to the poor and needy. The rich will always have the upper hand in society as the poor acknowledge them as their betters. You should try the Shrimp Scampi. It really is top of the line."

"Are you ready to place your order?" a well-dressed waiter asked, standing by their table.

"Yes, we will both have the Shrimp Scampi and a bottle of Dom Perigon."

"Hold up there, Waiter Man." Rayford stops him as he prepares to write down the order. "She can have the shrimp. I'll have some Jambalaya and a bottle of Corona with a wedge of lime and a straight-up shot of your best Scotch."

"Of course, Sir." He backs away with a smile.

"Why do you always insist on embarrassing me? I am trying to teach you how to train your palate to enjoy good food instead of mediocre slop."

"Don't bother. I like my slop. It suits me."

"Obviously." She looks around the room at the well-dressed people enjoying their meal. "I feel like a low-life. I am not dressed to dine at such a fine restaurant."

"Not your fault. You haven't had a chance to unpack. We're fine. We're both too tired to worry about going shopping. I'm sure we're not the only tired travelers to come into this place, not wearin' designer duds."

The waiter places a wine glass down on the table in front of Regina, then lifts a bottle of champagne from an ice bucket, and quickly wraps a linen towel around the bottle before pouring a small amount of the wine into her glass. Regina allows the bubbles to settle to the bottom before lifting the glass to her mouth.

"I sure hope you intend to drink more'n that for what that bottle of vinegar is gonna cost ya," Rayford laughs outright.

Regina sips from her glass, then smiles. "Yes, this is a fine vintage."

The waiter proceeds to fill her glass two-thirds of the way full before turning to set a shot glass filled with Scotch and a bottle of beer on the table in front of Rayford. A small plate of lime wedges is placed near the bottle.

"Thank you," Rayford tells the waiter before picking up his glass. "Here's to our lives takin' a sharp turn for the better here, Regina."

Without thinking, Regina smiles, lifting her glass in a toast.

Rayford drinks the Scotch all in one drink, then smiles. "I gotta admit. That's the best Scotch I've ever had the pleasure of enjoyin. Sure beats the hell outta bar Scotch. I guess there's something to be said for bein' able to afford the best.

Regina nods as she enjoys her glass of wine.

As the waiter sets their food down on the table in front of them, Rayford leans forward. "Before you get too busy, I'll have a double shot of that fine Scotch and another beer."

"Of course, Sir. I will bring your order right away."

"They sure are polite here."

"Of course, they are polite. They want to receive a generous tip."

"Let me ask you something, Regina. Have you ever just let yourself relax and enjoyed yourself?"

"Certainly, I have. I am very wealthy, so, therefore, I can afford to have the best the world has to offer. Only those who are poor have to say things they don't mean and be nice to those they could not care less about." She took a small bite of her food and smiled.

"Have you ever been laid by a real man?"

Regina's fork drops to her plate as she stares over at him. "You will keep a civil tongue in your mouth if you know what is good for you and if you want to keep your job!" She hissed her threat, looking around the room to be sure they had not been overheard.

"No, I'm serious." He leans towards her. "Have you ever been with a man who wants to be with you because you're a beautiful and desirable woman?

"Of course I have." She looked away as she spoke.

"I think you're lyin'. I think you've only been with pretty boys who want to better their station in life. They tell you what they think you want to hear and treat you like a cold China Doll." Rayford finished the last of his meal, and after wiping his mouth on the white linen napkin, dropped it down on his plate.

"I think you have had too much to drink, and if I don't want to be embarrassed, I am going to go up to my room." She scoots back her chair, almost running into the waiter who is laying a black leather folder on the table. Quickly, Regina sits back in her chair and opened the folder to withdraw the bill. After scribbling her name, she wrote in what she was leaving for a gratuity then withdrew her credit card from her wallet, putting both the card and the bill back inside the folder.

"Thank you, Ma'am. I'll be right back with your card."

"I hope you were generous. He had to run back and forth a few times," Rayford tells her, a big grin covering his handsome face.

As Regina stands up, the waiter lays her card down on the table. Without a word, Regina places the card in her purse and turns to leave.

"Hold up," Rayford downs the last of his bottle of beer and, getting a little unsteadily to his feet, walks away from their table.

Standing before the elevator door, Regina looks over at him. "If you ever embarrass me again, you can leave. I will not be thought of as white trash who keeps company with a sloppy drunk."

"Aw, for Christ's sake, woman, lighten up. We've had a long day. I'm tired from stackin' sacks of shit twice, enjoyin' a fine meal and a few drinks. With everything combined, the drinks have gone to my head.

As the doors to the elevator slid open, a well-dressed, attractive woman walks forward and seeing Rayford smiles up at him.

"Evenin', Miss," he said, giving her his best smile.

Regina sniffs and walks through the doors. Withdrawing her room key from her purse, she glances at the room number and then pushes the number for their floor.

"Glad to see not every woman finds me hard to look at."

"Probably a hooker. If you want, I can loan you a few dollars so you can continue having a good time." Regina smiles at him. "But that will come out of your pay."

"Thanks, that's very givin' of you, but that woman's got too much class for a hooker. That woman's a lady. Which proves my point. Not every woman who's rich is a bitch. Some can be a real nice individual."

Regina walks through the open door of the elevator and stomps down the long hall until she comes to her room. "Here," she threw his room key at him, "I'll say good night. Don't expect to see me before 10:am. I'm not an early riser, and after the day

I've had, it might be even later."

"I take it you don't want me to tuck you in." The smile he gives her, and the low timbre of his voice earns him a look of disgust for his trouble.

CHAPTER 12

The ringing of the phone brings Jack sitting upright in the bed. "Yeah."

"Good morning, Jack. Sorry to wake you, but we have a meeting with the top brass in a couple of hours, and I know how you like to be prepared."

"I take it we're gonna be discussin' the Hindel murder. Since we've done all we can do, then I guess the brass is ready to release the mansion as being a crime scene."

"Yeah. This should make Regina Hindel happy."

"Maybe, maybe not. She got a good look at what was out there that night. I wouldn't be surprised if she puts the place on the market and goes back to New Orleans."

"Couldn't blame her. But no one around here will buy that place. No one around here would take the place if she was giving it away."

"Oh, I am sure there are plenty of those in the parish who would jump on the chance to own the Hindel Mansion.

"Okay, are we gonna ride in together and who is picking up who?"

"I'll pick you up."
"I'll be ready."

***

Captain Stevens taps the ash from his cigar into an ashtray on the desk. "Hearing the news that another Hindel has moved back into the parish is very disturbing, to say the least. Thought we were through with all that foolishness." He leans back in his swivel chair, stretches his short legs out in front of him.

Donavan looks at the man seated across from him, dressed in a black suit, blue silk tie, white shirt and black dress shoes, and tries not to laugh as he sees his eyebrows rise with distaste at Jack's black, western cut suit coat, dark blue shirt unaccompanied by a tie and black cowboy boots.

"The two individuals we had to kill in the mansion were hiding in a secret room." Donavan glances down to make sure his own dress suit is still looking good. "There is no telling how many more rooms are there that don't show up on the blueprints."

"You say that only one of the perpetrators was named Hindel?"

"Yes, sir. The other was going by the name of Romanitti. There is a woman who has a large estate in the parish who is also named Romanitti. Detective Olivier' and I went to see her and tell her that she may have had a relative killed on the Hindel Estate. Since she admits the name Romanitti is not a common name, she has agreed to pay for his disposal. I would guess she will go with having him cremated."

"Do you feel that the two you had to kill were Rougarous?"

At the same time, both Donavan and Jack nodded.

"Seems impossible that in this day and age, we could be sitting here discussing a monster such as a Rougarou and still be deemed to be in control of our faculties.

"What do you propose we do about this starting up again, Captain Stevens?"

"Surprised you don't have any ideas, Jack," he laughs openly.

"I do, but Donavan doesn't think you will go for it," Jack replies.

Captain Stevens leans forward to pick up the pitcher of ice water sitting on a tray with glasses. "Anyone else need a refresher?"

Jack turns two glasses upright. "Sure."

"Are you still off the booze, Jack?" Stevens fills all three glasses.

"I have a drink now and then. Nothing like before and nothing I can't handle." Jack's voice takes on a steely edge.

"I'm not trying to bring up any past problems. I can tell by looking at you, you have your act together. So let's hear your idea on what we have going on again in the parish."

"I think any time a Rougarou is found that the deputies should open fire and shoot their heads off. This way, they can't return to human form."

For a moment, Captain Stevens remains silent, then he nods. "I think you are absolutely right, Jack. Before, when one of them was wounded, it just slithered off to lick its wounds and then later return to do more harm. I am going to order that a memo be put out for everyone in the Sheriff's Department. When anyone comes up against a Rougarou, they are to shoot its head off."

Donavan replied, in all seriousness. "I am glad to hear someone speak up on what can be done to stop this. Although, I must admit I never thought the one who would see this problem for what it is would be someone at the top."

Stevens looks at them both, then looks away. "It's easy to laugh and make fun of something that we only see in the movies. However, when it happens closer to home, it's not so easy to laugh off."

Jack draws in his breath to speak, then remains silent as Donavan gives him a warning glance.

"Yes, well," Stevens rose to his feet, "I guess we have said all there is to say on the matter. I'll let the two of you go about your business and get on dealing with mine."

Donavan and Jack stand and are turning to leave when Stevens holds up his hand, stopping them.

"One more thing. You said you have no idea how many more secret rooms are in the mansion, right?"

"Yes. Not even on the blueprints. Since we have no idea who could be a part of this mess, I doubt it would do any good to try and find out," Donavan said.

"I hear you. Anymore it could be anybody."

"I suggest we get the K9s busy going over the entire place. The Hindel woman will be wanting to get moved in now that the place is no longer a crime scene.

"Do all you can to see the place is secured before you hand it over to her."

***

"Guess we will be spending some time out at the mansion with the K9s all day," Donavan said.

"That we both have wives is a mystery, given the small amount of time we spend with them."

"Damn good thing we're both studs, or they'd be looking elsewhere."

"You're gettin' more like me every day, partner." Jack laughs as he stoops to get into the jeep.

CHAPTER 13

Regina padded out of the bathroom, followed by billowing steam from the hot shower she had been enjoying.

Pulling the soft white robe she had been given upon checking into the hotel from the hook on the door, she slips it over her nakedness just in time to hear a tap on the door.

Tying the belt around her waist, she opens the door to find the two detectives she had been having such a difficult time with smiling at her.

"Yes?"

"Can we come in? We won't stay long," Donavan informs her.

"As you can see, I am not dressed, so whatever you have to tell me, you can say it here," Regina tells them in a harried tone of voice.

"You'll be happy to hear we will soon have the mansion ready for you to move into. We want to have the K9s go through the house to make sure there are no more secret rooms hiding flesh-eating Rougarous."

"Was that meant to be a joke, detective? If so, I fail to see the humor."

"What Detective Hays is tryin' to tell you, Miss Hindel is the Hindel Mansion is not someplace you want to be."

"The Hindel Mansion is going to be my home. I can't very well not be there," she said, stepping back so they could come into the room.

Donavan and Jack sit down in the only two chairs available, leaving Regina to seat herself on the side of the large bed.

"Miss Hindel, given what you and your hired hand saw the other night at the mansion, do you still feel you should live there?" Donavan watched her trying to discern how she was dealing with what she was being told.

"I think all that nonsense, about monsters killing people, is just that. The girl that was killed was killed by a wild animal. No human being is going to rip someone's throat out."

"You're right about that. No human being is going to rip someone's throat out. And this is why you should think long and hard about foregoing your living in the mansion. You saw the two that were there. Are you going to deny that?"

"I was tired and angry, and I was told a girl had been murdered on my estate. That would be enough to make anyone see things that really were not there."

"Come on, Donavan. She ain't gonna listen to anything we have to say. She's been warned, and that's all we can do."

"All right." Donavan stands up from the chair. "We should be through with the estate by this time tomorrow. At that time, you can move into the mansion. All I can say is, good luck."

"Thank you for your concern, detective. Now I can contact the movers, and let them know they can deliver my furniture as soon as possible. I am sure my hired hand and I will be fine."

"If I was you, Miss Hindel, I'd be sure and keep your

hired man close. Never know who might come knockin' in the middle of the night. And he looks like he could handle just about anything."

"Rayford will be staying in the cottage. He is my hired hand, not the paid stud you are implying he is.

"Come on, Jack, we have work to do. And I am sure Miss Hindel would like to finish getting dressed." Donavan walks to the door then turns. "Miss Hindel, we are not trying to frighten you with talk of the danger you can encounter by living in the mansion. We are trying to tell you, you and the man who will also be living on the estate will be in extreme danger every moment of the day and night you are there."

"Thank you for coming, detectives. I will be awaiting your call telling me when I can move into my home."

As the door closes behind them, Donavan and Jack stand for a moment, trying to understand why their warnings about a house that has already been the scene of numerous murders are being ignored, and all they can do is shake their heads as they make their way down the hall.

"I sure hope you're here to give the go-ahead 'bout movin' onto the estate. I'm ready to get the hell outta here and into a place I can call my own," Rayford Seals says, coming towards them down the hall.

"Yes, we just gave Miss Hindel the news that as soon as we have the K9s check out the entire estate and hopefully find it clean, you both will be able to move in. However, I did try and talk her out of moving into the mansion. Since it has already been the scene of more than one horrific murder, I want her and now you to be aware of what you are letting yourselves in for." Donavan tells him.

"I think we'll be all right. I don't run around unarmed, so

anything that tries to roll up on us will get a big surprise."

"Okay then. But let me give you a word of advice, Slick. If you do have the misfortune of meeting up with some Rougarous, be sure and shoot their heads all the way off. That way, they will have less chance of comin' back to life after they change back to human form," Jack said, slapping the other man on the shoulder before heading off down the hall.

"If you had given me that advice before we saw what we saw, I would of told you to go and see a shrink. Now? While I want to get into a place that doesn't have hordes of people in and out, I have to admit, I'm not anxious to jump into livin' on that estate."

"Too bad your boss lady ain't as smart. She thinks now that what the two of you saw out there was all in her imagination.

For a moment, his eyes mirrored the fear he felt at the memory of the grotesque faces staring out at them a short distance away the night he and Regina had thought to sneak onto the estate and spend the night instead of staying in a flea-infested motel. "Yeah," he replied, his voice low and without the usual bravado, "she's a looker, but you're right, she ain't too smart."

"We gotta get to work, so all I can tell ya, Seals is, good luck."

Seals nods, then continues on down the long hall.

***

Regina finishes buttoning her blouse, then voices an angry curse as she hears a tapping on the door. "What is it now?" She yanks open the door. Her hostility turns quickly to that of surprise as Rayford stands in front of her.

"Are you going to invite me in?"

"Yes, come in." She moves to the side as he brushes past her.

Without waiting to be told, he seats himself in one of the chairs. "Do you want to order us up some drinks, or should I?"

"I am not going to allow you to get drunk."

"I ain't plannin' on gettin' drunk." His voice took on a sharp edge. "I would like to kick back with a few drinks. I got things on my mind."

"All right." She called down to the desk and ordered some drinks to be sent up to the room. "Now, what is getting you upset this time?"

"I just talked to the two detectives who told you we can get into the mansion maybe tomorrow if their search dogs don't find anything wrong on the estate."

"Yes, so?"

"I ain't so sure we should live there. And the detectives agree."

"I don't have time for this nonsense. I am the owner of the Hindel Mansion, and I intend to live there. If you are too much of a coward to stay there, then let me know right now so I can find a replacement for you.

Rayford jumps up and grabs her by her shoulders. "Now you listen to me. There ain't a goddamn cowardly bone in my body. But unlike you, I don't run around with my head up my ass, ignoring danger!"

"You're hurting me," she whispers, her voice filled with more than a little fear as she tries to back away from him.

"Believe me, what's out there'll hurt you a hell of a lot more'n I ever would." Rayford releases her to drop back down in his chair.

Regina sits down in a chair across from him. "Do you really think we will be in danger if we live on the estate?"

"Do you remember what we both saw out there?" Rayford

gets to his feet as they heard a tap on the door.

"You called down for an order from the bar?" The man, holding a tray filled with an ice bucket, two glasses, a bottle wrapped with a linen towel, and a bottle of scotch, asked.

"Yeah, thanks a lot. You can go ahead and put this on Miss Hindel's tab." He sets the tray down on the wet bar sitting against one wall. "I'll let you do the honors. I watched all you had to go through before drinkin' this stuff. Ya need to learn to drink good scotch."

In spite of herself, Regina smiles. "I can see I might as well give up on teaching you to enjoy good wine."

"Yes, you can. Now back to the situation at hand. I asked you if you remember what we both saw out there."

"I don't know if I really saw something or if you had me so scared that I thought I saw what you were seeing."

"All right. Just answer me this. What exactly do you think you saw?"

Regina takes a long drink from her glass of wine before answering his question. "I thought I saw two figures out in the swamp staring at us."

"All right. And what did those two figures you saw look like?"

Regina shuttered. They were tall and covered with fur, and their faces were very ugly and distorted."

"Did their faces look like an animal's face?"

"No," she whispered, meeting his stare, "their faces looked human."

"And you still want us to go and live there!" Rayford pours more scotch over the ice in his glass. "Woman, you beat all I've ever seen."

"That is my house!" Regina jumps to her feet. "Every blade

of grass on that estate belongs to me, Regina Hindel." She beats her fist against her chest.

"I am not arguing that fact. But it isn't safe." Rayford drains his glass, reaches for the bottle of scotch.

"The detectives said they were going to have their dogs go over the estate to make sure it was safe. If they don't find anything, then why would it hurt for us to live there?"

"Were you given the plat map on the estate? If you have that, we should be able to see any rooms that are there."

"They should be in all my papers. We can look them over when we get out to the mansion and see."

Rayford sets his glass of scotch down on the small bar and walks over to take Regina by her shoulders. "I know you want to live in the mansion. It's yours, and you have every right to be there. I just don't want you to be hurt. And, I don't want to be hurt either. We've heard a lot of bad things about that house. And they haven't all come from the detectives."

Without thinking, she reached out to run one hand down the side of his face. "Why don't we wait and see what the police dogs find? Maybe they will tell us the mansion is not habitable.

"Yeah, you could be right," he murmured, leaning in and pulling her head against his chest. "Now, I'll leave it up to you. Do you want we should go get something to eat, or do you want to order up lunch to eat here?"

"I think we should go and have lunch in the dining room." She leans back to look up at him. "We have both had a few drinks, so I think it would be better if we go and eat."

"Safer you mean." Rayford looks down at her, smiling.

CHAPTER 14

"Stop it!" Jack sets straight up in bed. "You need to stay the hell away from me!"

"Jack, what in god's name is wrong? Are you having another bad dream?" Seelah tried to gather him into her arms.

Without answering, Jack yanks away from her and, throwing back the covers, gets to his feet to stomp off to the bathroom.

Seelah could hear the shower come on, and without thinking about what she is going to do, she gets out of bed to follow him, naked, into the bathroom.

Jack stands beneath the spray of cold water. He jumps as he feels slender arms come around his waist.

"Jack, you need to tell me what is going on. These dreams you are having are not normal."

"I'm not havin' bad dreams." His voice is low. "I'm bein' visited and hit on."

"What do you mean you are being hit on? Are you saying the person is making sexual overtures towards you?" Seelah remembers the beautiful blond haired woman in Jack's dream, and she tries to keep her voice soft and unaccusatory.

"Yes. The woman who keeps comin' into my dreams to try and have sex with me is Jillianna Romanitti.

"The woman you said claims you and she were lovers in a past life."

"She also claims we had a child together. A little girl that she had to give up in order to save the girl's life."

"What happened in a past life is just that, a past life. It should not have any bearings in this life."

"She seems to think it does. How can I make her leave me alone? When Donavan and I went to see her the other day to tell her about one of her relatives who was in need of a burial, I told her I knew what was goin' on and for her to stay away from me. I come close to knockin' the hell outta her."

"I can't blame you there," Seelah said, her voice taking on an angry tone.

Jack turns around to pull her against him. "My little She-Cat. I like it when you get jealous of me. Makes me know you want me all to yourself."

Seelah smiles, running her hands over his chest then, leans forward to bite his erect nipple, bringing a deep moan from his throat. "Jillianna Romanitti may have started your arousal, but I am the woman who will bring it to completion."

Jack laughs outright as Seelah jumps up to wrap her slender legs around his waist.

Jack enters her slick tightness with a sharp flick of his hips. "There is only one woman who can cool the raging fires burning inside my body. And she is right here in my arms where she belongs."

"No other will ever satisfy you like I can, my love." She rotates her hips faster and faster until she feels hot liquid spew forth inside her hungry body, quickly followed by the rhythmic beat of his cooing desires. A low-pitched moan leaves her throat as she feels her own hot juices explode inside her.

Jack pulls her close as she unwinds her legs from around his waist.

"How did I ever make it this far in my life without your love, my beautiful wife? The gods have really smiled on me to bring you into my world."

"They have smiled on both of us, my love. And now that they have, I will never allow anyone to come between us."

"Seelah, do you think you can stop what is happenin' in my dreams?" Jack's voice is filled with both hope and unease. "Are you strong enough in your gifts to stop a woman who is not only a vampire but someone who has lived on this earth for many years?"

"There is only one way to find out, Jack. But, if I find I am not strong enough, I know someone who is."

"You're talkin' 'bout Chandra." Jack turns away.

"Yes, I am. Chandra is our friend, and I know she will come to help us if I call her."

Silently, Jack picked up a bar of soap to wash away the sweat from off his body. He ducks his head, allowing the water to rinse away the lather.

"Jack, I said Chandra is our friend. You don't have to be afraid or embarrassed to talk about her. Your relationship with her was before we got together."

"Yeah," he gave a slight laugh, "we could say the same thing 'bout Jillianna Romanitti and look at the mess that's caused."

Seelah turns her back to him and flattens the palms of her hands against the wall, smiling as Jack runs the bar of soap over her back and arms, then down further to elicit a slight giggle to fall out into the silence.

A slight tap on the door has them staring at each other.

"Yes," Jack calls out. "Who is knocking on my door? Is he friend or is he foe?"

"It's your son, Donnie. His voice is filled with more than a little fear. "I can't find Mama. Do you know where she is?"

"Mama is here with me, Donny."

"What are we going to do? We neither one brought a robe."

Jack holds up his hands for silence. "Mama will be down to fix breakfast in a moment, Donny. Will you do us a favor and get out the juice so it will be ready to pour when we come down?"

"Yes, I can do that."

They hear a happy twitter as he runs from the room to do as he was asked.

"We are going to keep a robe hanging on the inside of the door from now on," Seelah laughs aloud. "That was too close."

"I agree." Jack reaches out as Seelah steps from the shower. "Thank you for being here for me this morning. I think that between us, we can get through what is going on with Jillianna Romanitti."

"I know we can, Jack, and I will be talking with Chandra for backup. I have been blessed with my ability to see and feel with my psychic gifts, and I do not take them for granted, but Chandra is much more powerful than I am."

"Chandra was given her psychic gifts by Jonathan Hindel. I would think that a gift coming from God would be a lot more powerful than something that was given by someone as evil as Hindel." His tone takes on a sour note.

Seelah looks at him, knowing he has suffered at the hands of both Chandra and Jonathan Hindel. She runs a gentle hand over his chest. "In the end, Chandra only used her gift for good. And in so doing, God allowed her the right to keep her gift. I think our Holy Father is the one who should have the last word in this discussion."

"Now, that makes sense. And since she is now on the side of good, I feel a lot better at letting you interact with her."

"Thank you for your permission, oh masterful one." She smiles, letting him know her words are meant in jest.

"I love you, Seelah, and I never want to lose you. If I can keep you and Donny safe, I will be a happy man."

"Speaking of Donny, we better take this time to run for our robes before he comes looking for us."

"I'm right behind you, my wife."

Some distance away, an angry Jillianna Romanitti sits in a chair on the patio as she goes over the images in her mind.

"You will pay for turning me away while you make love with your other woman. It should be me you hold close and make love with. It should be me who makes your body burn with desire. I am the one who bore our child. A child we never got to raise. It is not fair you are able to share a child with another woman. You need to come back to me, Karleto. You need to share my bed and let me satisfy your body as no one else can. Soon you will see this is how it must be. You will see we belong together just like before. For now, I will be content to remember how it was when you made love with only me."

CHAPTER 15

"Hurry up, Rayford, the movers will be here any moment, and I want to show you the rest of the house before they get here." Regina throws open the door.

Trying to keep a positive outlook, he walks through the front door of the mansion. "Not a bad lookin' shack." He glances around. "Have you seen all of the house?"

"No, she laughed, running into the large kitchen, "As I told you before, I had only made it through the door when the detectives stopped me and let me know I was going to have to leave, and this time I wanted to wait until you could check it out with me." She pulls open the impressive side-by-side refrigerator and freezer. "Lawrence Hindel certainly knew how to furnish a kitchen. I have seen only the best and most expensive appliances."

"Long as there was a big price tag attached, you're impressed."

"Stop it. I am not going to let you ruin this day for me with your sour attitude."

A loud buzzer sounds off to the side of the room.

"That would be the movers at the gate." She runs over to

press a button on the intercom. "The gate will swing open in a moment, and you can drive through."

"This place is already filled with furniture. You're going to have a hard time puttin' more in here."

"What pieces I don't want you can have moved down to the cottage. Why should you bother when this is what they get paid for?"

"The cottage is pretty well full already. But yeah, I could probably use some more. Especially some of the bedroom furniture. We can check out what the furniture looks like in some of the guest rooms. Maybe no one used the bed in some of those."

"Don't start. I am having a happy time, and you will not ruin it for me," she tells him, trying to keep the anger out of her voice.

They walk outside as the truck pulls up in front of the mansion.

Two men get out of the truck. The man on the passenger side has a clipboard. "We'll need you to sign these forms, Madame, sayin' you received your furniture and that it is not damaged in any way." He hands the clipboard out to Regina."

"I am not signing anything until I see for myself the furniture is undamaged." She holds up her hands, palms outward. "A Lot of the pieces are very expensive."

"Yes, Madame, whatever you say." His tone of voice is less than respectful.

Regina's eyes narrow as he walks away.

"Okay, let's get started movin' all this inside." Rayford walks over to the back of the truck.

"Rayford, you don't need to help. This is what they get paid for."

"They drove all night to get here. I know how much you

enjoy using that phrase, but the way I see it is, the sooner they get done, the sooner we can have the house to ourselves." He winks at her and was surprised to see a slight smile touch her full mouth.

They work through the morning and into the afternoon until the last piece of furniture is set down in its place.

"This is one helluva house you got here, dude," the younger of the two men says. "Man, I'd give anything to own a place like this."

"Things ain't always what there're cracked up to be," the driver of the truck says.

"Aw, don't mind, James. He's a weirdo."

"What do ya mean, he's a weirdo?" Rayford walks over closer.

"He sees things that ain't there. He creeps people out. But I gotta tell ya, the things he tells ya that are gonna happen, do."

"You're sayin' he's a psychic."

"Yeah, I guess that's what you'd call him."

"I'm gonna need the two of you to do me a favor."

"Sure, what do ya need?"

"I need some of the furniture in the house moved down to the small cottage you passed on your way up to the mansion."

"Come on, Bob, we need to get the hell outta here and get back on the road," James tells him, coming back to the truck.

"Hold up there, James. I was just tellin' your partner here, I'm gonna need some furniture moved from the mansion to the cottage down the lane."

"Naw, we gotta get back on the road, man."

"There'd be an extra $50.00 in it for ya."

"All right, but let's get on it. We still have a long ways to go before sundown."

The three men walk into the bedroom.

"Okay, what all do you need moved?" James asked.

"I'm gonna need this bed and the chest of drawers and this nightstand." Rayford looks around the room. "That should do it."

James grabs onto the mattress, preparing to heft it onto the dolly, when he steps back, his face drained of color.

"Oh shit," Bob murmured, "here we go again."

"What's wrong? Are you havin' some kinda attack?" Rayford put his hand on the man's shoulder, only to have him jerk away.

James stumbles backwards. "It ain't human." His breath is coming faster and faster as his eyes stare out at something only he can see. "So much blood! She's only a little girl! You filthy sick bastard, leave her alone!!" James sinks to his knees. The sobs coming from his throat make him gasp for breath. "Leave her alone." His voice is little more than a whisper now as he covers his face with his hands in an attempt to hide what he is seeing.

"Whatever is going on in here?" Regina says, running into the room. "Were the three of you fighting?"

"No." Rayford pulls her out of the room and down the hall.

"I want to know what is going on."

"Accordin' to Bob, James is a psychic who sees things. Guess he saw something that's happened in the room we was gettin' ready to remove the bed from."

"Oh, for Pete's sake. I do not need this silliness in my house." Regina starts to walk back down the hall when Rayford takes hold of her arm.

"No, you need to leave him alone. He was not pretendin' to see somethin'. He did see somethin'. And what he saw doesn't bode well for us to want to stay here."

"People can't see things that aren't there. Only people who are mentally ill. You can be sure I will be calling his boss to report how he acted here."

"No, you will not." He pulls her towards the bedroom they had just vacated. "You're gonna come back in this room and take a good hard look at this man. Then, you are going to let him tell you what it was he saw. And I warn you, Regina, if you dare be rude to him, I will walk out of this house, and you can have it all to yourself."

Without another word, they walked into the room to find the two men standing off to the side.

"Sorry 'bout that. Sometimes things get to me. Things I have no control of. Guess I can expect a call to the company about what happened here today."

Rayford nudges Regina non too gently with his elbow.

"No, I will not be calling your company." She keeps her eyes cast downward.

"I want you to tell us exactly what you saw in this room. And don't leave anything out. We are gonna be livin' in this house, and we need to know what the hell we're up against here."

"Okay, but remember you asked me." He stood for a moment, looking at the two waiting for him to tell them what he had seen. "What I saw wasn't human."

"What did it look like, James?" Rayford keeps his voice low and even.

"What I saw was a monster. It was covered in short black fur, and its hands were claw-like. But the worst part is, it had the face of a human. The face was covered in short dark fur, but it was a human face."

"I heard you say somethin' 'bout a little girl. What was

that about?"

"He was eating the flesh of a child. There was blood everywhere. I could hear the sounds he made. Slurping and ripping." James' face showed the horror he was feeling in telling what he saw. "Thank God, she was already dead. Her throat was ripped out, and he was licking her blood."

Rayford looks over at Regina, and without thinking, he pulls her close against his hip.

"All right. I think we've heard enough."

"Yes," she whispered, "I think we've heard enough."

"We should get this furniture moved to where you need it to be."

You can move the dresser and the nightstand, but you can leave the bed. Rayford pulls two twenties and a ten from his wallet to hand it to James.

"Thanks." He accepts the bills, putting them in his shirt pocket. "I think allowin' me to tell you what I saw has helped to get it outta my mind. And for this, I am much obliged. I would suggest you call in a Catholic Priest to come and bless this house." He looks at them pointedly. "And if I was you, I'd give some serious thought to vacating this house."

Rayford tightens his hold on Regina.

"There's so much evil here that I don't know if even a priest can get rid of all the negativity. Anyway, Bob and I need to get goin', so let's get on with gettin' this furniture moved. I might feel all right now, but I'll tell ya, once I'm outta here, I ain't plannin' on ever comin' back."

CHAPTER 16

Donavan looks over at Jack as they sit, going over all the paperwork from the crime scene investigation. "Says here, the deceased was a fourteen-year-old female."

"Makes you wonder why parents'd allow their daughter to be out runnin' loose at such a young age."

"Yeah. Goes back to when teens were partyin' on the Hindel Estate when they thought no one lived there."

"Until they had the misfortune to run into Lawrence."

"We should have been the detectives to handle this case, but I have to tell you, I'm glad we've climbed up in ranks so we can turn down a case if we feel like it. Besides, we did our share with Jonathan and Lawrence and Rafael. I think we've earned having this one go to other detectives. I don't even like going over the paperwork, but maybe we can find out why the girl was on the property. Listen to this. It says here that when the girl's parents were notified about their daughter being found dead on the grounds of the old Hindel Mansion, they were as clueless as the officers as to why she was there. When they went to bed that night, they said their daughter was in her room.

"Sounds to me like she had a late-night date with somebody.

"Yeah, and that somebody is a somebody her parents had no idea about. So, we don't know any more than we did before we started reading the reports.

Donavan put all the papers back in the folder and laid it to the side of his desk. "I guess since the K9s didn't find anything pointing to any more hidden rooms, I feel safe in letting Regina Hindel and her handyman move into the mansion."

"I don't think I'd use the word safe. We both know there's no way in hell the Hindel woman and Seals are safe out there. Even if Rougarous ain't lurkin' on the inside of the mansion, they're sure as hell lurkin' around the grounds and the swamp."

Donavan looks up as a tap sounds on the office door. He motions the man standing there to come in.

"Lieutenant Hays, there are two people here to see you. A Miss Regina Hindel and a Mr. Rayford Seals. Mr. Seals says it's urgent they speak with you."

"Hmm, this could be interesting," Jack sits forward in his chair.

"Show them in, deputy."

"Miss Hindel, Mr. Seals. What brings you to the sheriff's department? I hope there's no problem with the mansion." Donavan holds out a hand to each of them before directing them to be seated.

"I guess there could be. In any event, we're in need of your help," Rayford replies.

"We'll be glad to help you any way we can," Jack tells him.

"My furniture was delivered today, and one of the movers, who claimed to be a psychic or whatever they like to call themselves, had some very strange things to say about what he says he saw in one of the bedrooms," Regina speaks up.

"Correct me if I'm wrong, Miss Hindel, but I take it you ain't too keen on psychics," Jack said, looking closely at her.

"No, I am not. I believe they are charlatans."

"I don't know if I am or not, but I gotta tell ya, whatever it was James, he was the one to see somethin', was seein' he sure as hell was not makin' it up," Rayford tells them.

"What did he say he saw?" The chair Donavan is sitting in squeaks as he leans forward.

"He said a monster was eatin' the flesh of a little girl and lickin' the blood from where her throat had been ripped out." Rayford shuttered in fear.

Jack put a hand on his shoulder. "Rayford, did he describe the monster?"

Rayford nodded. "Yeah." His tone lacks its usual in-your-face bluster. "He said it was covered in short dark fur, and it had the face of a human."

"Rougarou," both Donavan and Jack say at once.

"They fed on the bodies of the children in this parish for years," Jack delivers, getting to his feet.

"I hope you are not going to bring my relatives into this again because if you are, I am leaving." She uncrosses her legs, plants both feet flat on the floor.

"Then you best hit that door because the Hindels are largely responsible for the infestation of Rougarous in this parish," Jack said, expecting to hear Rayford's usual onslaught of anger on Regina's behalf and was surprised to see him sitting quietly and staring off into the room.

"Mr. Seals, are you all right? You look a little shaken up," Donavan says.

"What? Oh yeah, I just can't wrap my mind around what

James saw."

"Or, said he saw. Rayford, I can't believe you feed into all this silly gibberish," Regina laughs slightly.

"Miss Hindel, I think you're the one who needs to wake up. We're trying to tell you that the Hindel Estate is a very dangerous place. But you won't listen." Donavan stares at her. "You said you came here in need of help. What kind of help are you looking for?"

"My delivery man seems to think I need to call in a Catholic Priest to bless my house. I think he is being overly dramatic.

"Since we ain't from around here, we need you to tell us where we can find a Catholic Priest who will help us," Rayford says.

"I'll be glad to call one of the Catholic Churches and speak with a priest," Donavan told him.

"Do you think that can really work?" Rayford asked.

"I guess all we can do is try."

"If you're smart, Miss Hindel. You'll put that goddamn estate on the market and take what you can get out of it and go back to New Orleans," Jack tells her.

"I think the detective's right, Regina."

"Well, I don't think he's right. That estate belongs to me, and I am not giving it up just because of some voodoo nonsense."

"So where are we on this? Do you want the help of a Catholic Priest to bless the mansion or not?" Donavan interrupts.

"Yes, we do," Rayford said. "Regina, you can laugh and make fun all you want, but I believe James saw somethin' that happened in that house, and I, for one, don't want to be the next victim of whatever the hell it was."

"I think you are being wise, Mr. Seals, in dealing with this problem, and make no mistake, both you and Miss Hindel do have a problem." Donavan looks over at Regina to get her take on what he had just told Rayford Seals.

Getting to her feet, Regina slings the long strap of her purse over her shoulder. "When you are finished playing games, Rayford, I will be waiting in the car."

"She is one commanding young woman, Seals. You got your hands full. You got her to put up with, and who knows how long it will be before the Hindel Rougarous decide to move back into the mansion, if they haven't already," Jack grins over at him.

"If you're tryin' to piss me off, you might as well give it up, that shit with James shocked all the fight right outta me."

"At least now you know we weren't tryin' to feed you a bunch of bullshit."

"Well, hell, guess I better get out there. If she has to wait five minutes, she'll have my nuts in a sling the rest of the day."

"I don't envy ya, partner. In the meantime, we'll see what we can do with findin' you a priest with enough balls to take on the Hindel Mansion."

"I appreciate it, and if I come off as an asshole earlier, I apologize." He holds out his hand to both detectives before heading out the door.

"That poor bastard," Jack laughs openly, shaking his head. "And she ain't even sharin' the honey."

"I'm going to get on to finding a priest with nerve enough to go out there." He dials the number listed in the phone book for a Catholic Church. "I doubt he'll be able to do anything of use, but at least he may be able to slow down some of the negativity."

"This has been going on for at least two hundred years in the parish, and you think one visit from a priest, mumblin' a few words and blowin' some smoke around the room, is gonna get rid of all the evil out there?"

"Jack, where that evil house is concerned, your guess is as good as mine. But, at least Seals is trying to do something to change things." He holds up a hand as he hears someone on the other line acknowledge him.

"Saint Francis Catholic Parish, can I help you?" A woman's voice inquires on the other line.

"I sure hope you can, Madam. My name is Lieutenant Donavan Hays of the Saint Anthony Parish Sheriff's Department. Would it be possible to speak with one of the priests in the parish?"

"Yes, just one moment and I will go get Father to speak with you."

"Thank you, I'll hold."

"Hello, this is Father Green. Can I help you?"

"Hello, Father, this is Lieutenant Donavan Hays of the Saint Anthony Parish Sheriff's Department calling. I hope I'm not interrupting your dinner."

"No, you're fine. What can I do for you?"

"Someone in the parish is in need of a house blessing. However, they are not Catholic. Is this going to be a problem"

"No, we can do a blessing for anyone of any faith. What is the name of the family in need?"

The woman's name is Regina Hindel. She recently took ownership of the Hindel Mansion."

There is a long pause. Finally, the voice of the man he had been speaking with comes back on the line. "That is a house of much evil. When did she wish to have the blessing done on the house?"

"I would say as soon as possible. Would later this evening be too soon?"

"No, that is fine. I will be finished with the confessional by

8:pm this evening, and then I can go and do the blessing."

"Would it be all right if another detective and I join you at the house? I am sure you will agree, the Hindel Mansion is not a place you want to go to alone."

"Thank you, Detective Hays. I am strong in my belief that I will be safe in doing God's work, but a little extra protection never hurts. I will see you at the mansion at 9:pm this evening. Until then, Detective Hays."

Donavan hangs up the phone. "We're going to meet Father Green at the mansion this evening at nine o'clock. I don't think he's too thrilled about going out there."

"Hell, can you blame him? I'm not happy 'bout goin' back there. What he should be doin' is an exorcism on that fuckin', ghoul-infested shit hole."

"Guess I better let Regina and Seals know to expect a visit tonight."

"Lawrence can be glad he's dead. Otherwise, I'd be kickin' his skinny ass for havin' that goddamn place built back up again."

CHAPTER 17

A small, black, and compact car drives behind Donavan's jeep as they travel up the long lane leading to the Hindel Mansion.

"Looks like the good father's behind us." Jack gives a slight laugh as he turns in his seat.

"Yeah, he thinks like we do about safety in numbers." Donavan glances in the rearview mirror.

"I don't mind tellin' ya. This bringin' in a priest to get rid of the negativity out here could make things worse."

"Why do you say that?" Donavan glances over at him. "A blessing should make things better, not worse."

Jack shakes his head, then looks at him. "I take it, you haven't watched movies where every time a priest tries to kick out the demons that are fuckin' with the family, things get a lot worse. Things start flyin' through the air, and it gets real cold and all kinds of shit."

"That's only in the movies, partner. This is for real."

Jack remains silent, staring at him.

"Okay, I get your point. Everything about this damn house is like a movie."

"Thank you."

Donavan brakes the jeep in front of the closed gate. "Do you want to do the honors, or do you want me to?"

"I'll do it," Jack said, sliding out of his seat. He pushes the button on the intercom. "Saint Anthony Parish Ghost Busters are here."

Jack waves a welcome to the car behind them as the gate slides open.

They can see Regina and Rayford waiting for them on the front porch step.

"Our welcoming committee is here."

"Yep, just like in the movie. From here on out, things start to get wild." Jack gets out of the jeep quickly, followed by Donavan.

Regina watched a man dressed in black slacks, a black shirt with a white Roman collar and carrying a leather bag move towards them.

"Miss Hindel, Mr. Seals, this is Father Green," Donavan told them.

"Nice to meet both of you." Father Green holds out his hand to each of them.

"Thank you for coming, Father. We need all the help with this that we can get," Rayford says, taking the hand being offered to him.

"Yes, well, sometimes Satan thinks he has the upper hand, and we who know better have to come in and show him that he's wrong," Father Green says.

"I want you to know that I don't believe in any of this silliness. My hired man and these two detectives," she flutters a hand in the direction of Donavan and Jack, "think we need to do this, so I am going to allow them and you, your fun."

"I have no problem with your beliefs. Almost everyone thinks they are above having the supernatural enter into their lives until it does," Father Green speaks his words quietly, but with deep feeling.

"Guess we best get to it, Rayford." Jack walks up beside the man staring at the priest, completely mystified. "Do you want to do the honors, or do you want me to lead the way?

"You can go inside," Rayford said. "The rest of us will follow behind." He glances over to Regina, who nods.

Donavan steps behind Father Green and grins as he spies the butt of a gun sticking out of his belt. "I see you agree with Detective Olivier' and me," he says quietly, his voice hushed so as not to draw attention from the others. "You don't come to the Hindel Mansion unless you're packin'."

"Ghosts and demons are one thing. It's the live ones I don't trust behind me."

"I hear you."

"Would it be all right to clear the things off of this coffee table?"

"Here, let me do it." Rayford moves forward. "There ain't much here. It should all fit up here on the mantel."

"As none of that stuff is mine, you can simply throw it all in the trash," Regina tells him.

"I think you are being wise," Father Green speaks up, standing beside her. "The more negativity you get rid of in a house such as this, the less chance you will have bad energy lingering in the dwelling."

Regina spares him a brief glance before looking away.

"Take it all the way out to the garbage, Rayford," Jack said. "I'll help you."

"Father, I'm almost afraid to ask this question, but I want

to know the answer." Donavan walks over to him.

"Ask me whatever you wish." He continues with what he is doing.

"The blood of the innocent has bled into the soil of the Hindel Estate for over 200 years. Do you honestly believe a simple house blessing is going to make a difference in what can and can't continue to live on these grounds?"

The priest looks up at him. "As with all evil, Detective Hays, there must be a starting place to rid the body and all the surrounding area of its touch. We will do a blessing first, and if we find the blessing was not enough, then we will do more."

"I appreciate your candor. None of us here know what to expect, so we are putting our trust in you."

"No, my friend, you are not. You are putting your trust in our Holy Father, and He will not let you down."

As Jack and Rayford walk back into the room, the priest makes the sign of the cross in readiness to begin the blessing.

"Jesus Christ, as the son of our Holy Father and our Holy Mother Mary, we ask that you come into this dwelling and bless all here. Blessed be the name of the Lord. All here answer by saying Amen."

A chorus of Amens could be heard throughout the room, and as Rayford looked over at Regina, he could see her whisper her reply with the rest of those in the room.

Father Green opens a small bible, and removing a silk bookmark, he begins to read aloud passages of Scripture he has chosen.

Without warning, the sounds of someone crying filters out into the room.

Regina grabs onto Rayford's arm as he silently pulls her against him.

Father Green holds up a hand for all to remain calm and listen to the Scripture he continues to read aloud.

"Of all the protection God has given unto you, the most powerful is the protection of sincere love. May our Holy Father help to grow the love between a man and his wife and any children they bring into this dwelling.

The wailing becomes louder, seeming to fill the entire house

Again, the priest raises his hand for them to stay standing quietly as he raises his voice to drown out the high-pitched crying.

He makes the sign of the cross above the door. "Bless all who enter here, and bless all who leave this dwelling through this door. We ask that this be done through Christ our Lord.

Father Green moves from room to room in the house, descending down into the basement and up the stairs to the bedrooms and the attic, saying prayers and asking for God's love and protection and making the sign of the cross above each door throughout all of the Hindel Mansion.

The wailing is quiet now. As though those caught between this plane and the next are now free to continue on.

"We thank you, Oh Lord, for freeing your lost children to leave this dwelling to be with you and all the Holy Ones in heaven. We give you glory in Christ's name."

He closed the Bible placing it back in the small leather bag he has brought with him.

"So that should do it, right, Father?" Jack asks.

"We can hope that will do it, Detective Olivier'. I know I can't be the only one to feel a lightness in the room where a heaviness had been present earlier."

"You're right. There is a big difference here." Donavan comes forward. "Feels like when Seelah sent that little girl on who had been trapped here by Jonathan Hindel."

"I knew the night could not pass without my relatives being brought into the mix," Regina breathes, her voice quiet and shaky.

Father Green looks at the young woman standing off to the side, and he moves over to stand beside her. "Miss Hindel, I can't promise how long the calmness in this house will remain, but if you ever need me to come back, I am leaving my card with the number of the church so you can call me."

"Thank you, but I think I'll be fine. I'm not a strong believer in your God, so I won't bother to have you return."

The priest gazes at her for a long moment, then looks away. "I'll be going now. I've done all I can do here for the time being. However, I'm only a phone call away if you need me." He drew a card from his pants pocket to hold it out to Regina, and when she kept her arms at her sides, he hands the card instead to Rayford.

"Thank you, Father, and thank you for all you did this evening."

Jack walks forward to where Regina stands, watching the priest as he talks quietly with Rayford and shaking her head.

"I take it you don't approve of priests," Jack said.

"I am not into the silliness of the entire Catholic Cult."

"The Catholic Church is not a cult, Miss Hindel, and even you have to admit he did a lot of good here tonight."

"Yes, whatever. Rayford is the one who suggested we bring him here. It sure wasn't my idea. And anyone with half an ounce of sense knows all that crying was rigged. I don't know how the priest made it sound so real, but since there is no such thing as a ghost, we both know he is the one responsible for what we heard."

"Miss Hindel, I am surprised that you are this naïve. What you heard during the blessing was real. I don't care if you believe me or not. But, there is one thing I can promise you about this house, and that is if you and Rayford continue to live here, there will come a time when you can no longer stick your head in the sand and pretend all is well. What you heard was the wailing of trapped souls. I don't know 'bout you, but I prefer the souls caught in this house should move on. Not only for their peace of mind but yours. I don't particularly like having those I can't see watching me." Jack smiled, reaching out his hand to her. "Anyway, it's late, so I wish you a good and hopefully safe night, Miss Hindel. His hand holds her's for a brief moment.

Across the room, a wispy figure stands watching Jack's interaction with the beautiful young woman standing before him, and she smiles.

"I'm ready to get out of here, Jack. It's been an interesting night, to say the least." Donavan takes Regina's hand in his. "Miss Hindel, I will bid you a good evening."

Rayford moves forward, clasping each man's hand in his. "Thanks for all you did. We appreciate it."

"No problem. This is what we're here for," Donavan replies.

"A thank you would not be asking too much after all that was done on your behalf here tonight, Regina," Rayford quietly scolds her.

"Thank you, both." The smile did not meet her eyes.

"I am happy I have kept my energy attuned to yours, for now, I know my long search is at last over. I will not come to you this night, my love. Tonight, I will watch over our daughter," Jillianna Romanitti whispers as she watches Jack walk out the door of the Hindel Mansion.

CHAPTER 18

Later that morning, Jiallianna rises from her slumber, swinging her long and slender legs off the side of the bed. Picking up a long, blue-green Caftan from off the bottom of the bed, she slips her arms through the sleeves.

Walking outside, she stretches out in one of the lounge chairs pulled up beside a glass table on the patio. As her body begins to relax, she allows her thoughts to go back to the Hindel Mansion and center on the beautiful young woman who is the mirror image of her.

"At long last, I have found you. Your soul lives in the body of a Hindel. What a cruel joke for the universe to play on the two of us, my child."

She looks up, smiling as Baxter sat her coffee and juice down on the table beside her chair.

"Good morning to you, Mz. Jillianna. Ah trust you slept well.

"Good morning, Baxter. Yes, I slept well and awoke refreshed and ready to greet the day." She laces her fingers together, raising her arms above her head in a carefree manner.

"Ah's glad to see that big smile on your pretty face," Baxter tells her, a toothy grin spreading wide across his dark face. "Are you gonna want some breakfast pretty soon?"

"No, Baxter, I am going to be out for a while today. I will pick something up then."

"All right then, you have a good day, Mz. Jillianna." He turns to walk back inside the house. Glad to see her in such a good mood and planning her day away from the mansion.

***

Rayford walks down the wide staircase and into the kitchen. Within moments the scent of freshly brewed coffee fills the air.

"Rayford, while I appreciate you spending the night in the house, I would appreciate you not running around half-naked."

He smiles at her over his shoulder as he takes down two cups from the cupboard. "Why? You gettin' turned on?"

"I will not put up with that crude language in my house. You will show me the respect I am due as your employer, or you will not be welcome to come inside." She takes the cup from his hand.

"You didn't answer my question. And you never made it clear just exactly where inside I am not allowed to enter.

"Oh, you are incorrigible." She walks around him to pour herself some coffee.

Without a word, he holds out his cup. "I made it. The least you can do is share it."

Regina fills his cup and, without looking at him, turns away to set the coffee pot back on its burner.

"Why are you afraid to look at me? I've been told I'm not that hard on the eyes." Rayford keeps his voice soft and low.

"Rayford, you are wasting your time in trying to win me

over. My money is going to stay where it is. In my name and not shared with some too-lazy-to-earn-his-keep, playboy."

With calm ease, Rayford sets his coffee down on the table and, reaching out, he removes her filled cup from her hand. Then, without a word, he tips her chin upward, so she has no choice except to look at him. "Now, you hear me, Regina Hindel. I don't give a flyin' fuck 'bout your money, or your big mansion, or anything else you think I want. You hired me to take care of the grounds here, and this is exactly what I will do. You were the one who asked me to sleep in the guest room. Which I did. I did not spend the night to try'n get laid. I stayed because you asked me to and because you let me know you were more uncomfortable bein' alone in this house than you let on." He drops his hand, and after giving her one more long look, he picks up his cup of coffee and walks away.

Regina stands where he has left her. She can hear him climbing up the staircase, and after a few moments, she hears him come back downstairs to walk out the back door of the mansion.

"Hmm, he need not get all upset," she murmured. "I was only letting him know what to expect."

She turns to walk into the living room when the buzzer goes off, letting her know someone is at the gate. Slowly she walks over to push the button.

"Yes?"

"Hello, Miss Hindel. I have come to welcome you to the parish. Can I come inside the grounds?"

"Yes, of course."

Regina walks outside to await her visitor.

Driving slowly up to the mansion, Jiallianna looks over to see a well-built man with no shirt on walking down the lane.

"Now there's someone to keep in mind for a lonely

evening," she murmurs aloud.

Rayford glances at the woman driving by and tries to think why she looks so familiar before continuing on to the cottage.

Impressed with the teal-blue Jaguar convertible driving towards her, Regina tries to stay calm as she waits for the woman to step out of the car.

"Hello," Jillianna calls out, stepping to the cobblestoned driveway, her arms filled with roses and a large covered tray.

Regina moves forward to lift the roses from the woman's arms. "Let me help you. Goodness, you have a lot to carry."

"Thank you. It didn't seem all that much when I got them," she laughed. "My name is Jillianna Romanitti. And as I said, I've come to welcome you."

"Please, do come in. I will put these beautiful roses in some water, and you can unburden yourself with what else you brought."

"What a nice kitchen." She set the covered tray down on the small island surrounded by decorative, high stools.

"Thank you. I never met Lawrence Hindel, the last Hindel to live here, but I can see he had very good taste."

"The tray is filled with different kinds of fruits and cheeses," Jillianna tells her.

"Let's go out to the patio. It is a beautiful day. If you will bring the tray, I will pour us both a glass of white wine." Seated in lounge chairs with a small patio table placed between them, Regina looks over at her guest. "This is going to sound so strange, but for some reason, I feel as though I know you."

"I feel the same way. Sometimes people just take to each other."

"Thank you for coming to welcome me here. You are the first one to be nice to me. For some reason, the people of this parish think anyone with the name of Hinde has to be evil."

"Yes. I am going to be completely honest with you. I had two detectives come to my home to tell me that a relative of mine was shot and killed on this estate. Shot and killed by them, the detectives. While I did not know the man they killed, I did feel responsible for his burial since he was carrying an ID that showed he carried my last name."

Regina feels her heart begin to beat faster. "Why did they feel the need to kill him?"

"They said he and another man was responsible for the murder of a young girl who was killed right here on your property; that they found them hiding in a secret room inside the mansion. The IDs they found on their person identified them as having the last names of Romanitti and Hindel."

To Jillianna's utter shock, Regina threw back her head, laughing openly. "For a moment, I wasn't sure who I had invited into my home. You're telling me one of your relatives was shot and killed by two detectives right here in my own home had me a little upset."

"And why aren't you upset now?"

"Because I doubt that our relatives are responsible for that poor unfortunate girl's death. Her throat was ripped out. I doubt our relatives would do that. She was killed by a wild animal. I think the two men they found inside the house were probably hiding from the same animal that killed the girl."

"And I still believe they were killed by Rougarous just as the detectives said."

Jillianna looks up to see the same man she had seen earlier standing in the doorway. "Please introduce me."

"This is my handyman, Rayford Seals. Rayford, this lady's name is Jillianna Romanitti. Jillianna has come to welcome me to the parish."

Rayford comes forward with his hand outstretched. "I am glad to meet you, Miss Romanitti."

"Please, call me Jillianna, Rayford." Her voice lowered as she looked at him. "I have a feeling you and I are going to be friends."

"Did you forget something, Rayford?" A chill sounds in Regina's tone as she catches the interest in his eyes as his gaze continues to move over the shapely body of her guest.

"No." A slight grin spreads across his face. "I just wanted to make sure you are all right with a stranger comin' to the house. After all, we know how the people of the parish feel about you bein' a Hindel."

"You know I find this very strange. I have lived in the parish for many years, and I have never heard any rumors about the Hindel name or about Rougarous either, for that matter."

"You must live a very sheltered life, Jillianna. Every time we turn around, someone's all but comin' at us with a crucifix and holy water."

"I hear you. I've had to deal with that a few times in my life, too." Jillianna smiles up at him. "So, have the police found out who the girl was who was killed here on your property?"

"No. The police haven't told us anything. I don't mean to be cold, but the girl should not have been on the estate without permission. Just as her friends should not have, as I am sure she was not here alone. Had they not been trespassing, perhaps the animal who attacked her would not have been lurking around."

"The detectives said she was killed by Rougarous. Human saliva was found on her."

"Oh, for Pete's sake, Rayford, there is no such thing as a Rougarou. The detectives are delusional. Her throat was ripped out, which points to an attack by some animal. The next thing they will be trying to feed us is she was killed by a vampire."

Jillianna smiles.

"Did you say human saliva was found on her?" Jillianna moves forward in her chair. "How can that be, unless there is something inhuman we don't know about what is attacking people?"

"Jillianna, please don't tell me you believe in this backwoods folklore being bantered about in the parish." Regina gets to her feet to look out over the grounds. "I feel I have found someone here I can be friends with who is not only my monetary equal but who is also up to my station in life, and from what I have seen of the people of Saint Anthony Parish, you are a rarity."

Rayford walks over to the tray filled with the different fruits and cheeses. He plucks a bit of fruit and some odd-looking cheese off the tray to pop them into his mouth.

"Rayford, I am sure you have some work to get done, so we will not keep you," Regina says without turning.

"Now that you mention it, I do need to get into town and pick up those sacks of fertilizer we had to leave at the store. Since I'll be alone, the owner should be in a better frame of mind."

"Superstitious old coot. I hope there is another store we can get what we need. I don't do business with those who are disrespectful to me."

"You were treated with disrespect? Why?"

"Yes, when we first came into the parish. And all because my name is Hindel. We could not even get a room at first at a nice hotel. I was not allowed to stay on the estate because it was a crime scene."

"I'm sorry your first day here was such an ordeal. People can be so ill-mannered when they meet someone they find different from themselves."

Regina turns, and coming across the patio, she reaches out to take Jillianna's hands in hers. "Now you see why I feel I have known you before."

"Yes, Jillianna smiled. "I feel you and I will become close friends now that we have found one another."

Rayford stands watching the two women who are all but mirror images of one another. Without warning, he feels a cold chill, almost like an omen pass over him.

CHAPTER 19

The bathroom door opened accompanied by a billow of steam carrying the strong scent of Jack's favorite soap. Seelah glances over at him from the bed, smiling as he unwraps the towel from his waist to drop it to the floor.

"Nice floor show, my love," she giggles as she lays the book she has been reading down on the small bedside table.

Jack ignores her humor. "I'm surprised you haven't asked 'bout how the blessing, the good father did on the Hindel Mansion, came off." He pulls on a pair of pajama bottoms, foregoing the top. Stooping over, he scoops up the damp towel to disappear briefly into the bathroom.

The joyful mood in the room changed. "I try to keep the Hindel Mansion and its inhabitants separate from our life here."

"So do I, but that isn't always possible since, as a detective on the Saint Anthony Parish Sheriff's Department, I'm once again involved with our furry parish lunatics."

"Did the priest come up against much evil?" Seelah's voice was a mere whisper.

"We're talkin' 'bout the Hindel Mansion, Seelah, of course,

he came up against a lot of evil." Jack's tone shows his anger."

Seelah remains silent.

"I'm sorry." Jack blows a long breath from his lungs. "I don't need to take my frustration out on you."

"Jack, I'm getting the feeling that there is more going on here. Do you want to share with me what it is?"

"If I could, Seelah, I would. I think more is going on too, but for the life of me, I can't pinpoint what it is."

"Would you like me to help you figure it out?" Seelah sits up straight in the bed and flips the bed covers back so Jack can lie down.

"You might be able to lend a hand. I'm sure as hell not comin' up with any answers." He lays out straight on the bed and, taking a few deep breaths, as Seelah taught him to do when relaxing his mind, waits for her to begin.

"I feel your dreams and your bad mood of late has a lot to do with the Jillianna Romanitti woman. Is she the one you are seeing in your dreams? Just answer yes or no."

"Yes." Jack tries to remain calm and in a relaxed state.

"Are your dreams scrambled, or do they seem as though you are actually there, that what is happening in your dreams is real?"

"Yes." His tone of voice is showing anger.

"Stay calm, and let me find out why she is visiting you. What is it she is wanting you to do?"

Jack sits up in the bed, then gets to his feet. "I think you should be able to figure that out for yourself, Seelah."

"Yes, I know what she wants from you, but I want you to say aloud what she wants."

"She wants me to have sex with her! For Christ's sake, when a man wakes up with a boner after dreaming of being with a beautiful woman, what the hell else could she want?"

"You are not having dreams of Jillianna Romanitti. You are having visits from this Romanitti woman. She leaves her body to come to you."

"If that's the case, she would have to have an out-of-body." Jack stands by the bed staring at her. "How the hell can a spirit have sex?"

"You would be surprised what someone can do while they are out of their physical body." Seelah tries to keep the anger she is feeling out of her voice.

"Is she gonna be able to continue doin' this? Comin' into my dreams at night? I mean," he mops a shaking hand over his sweaty face, "can't you put a stop to it?"

"I think I can." Seelah smiles up at him.

"You are the woman I love, Seelah. I have no desire to be with another woman, and that goes for my dreams, too."

"Our love for one another is stronger than the mere desires of the flesh, Jack. For this woman to be able to have OBEs, she has to have psychic powers.

"What the hell's an OBE?"

"An OBE is an out-of-body experience. Chandra could leave her body and travel to other places. This Romanitti woman is able to come here and enter into your dreams."

"Wait a minute! She can actually come right here to our house? I don't want that evil bitch anywhere near you and Donny!"

"The next time she tries to come into your dream, I will give her a warning that if she does not leave and not come back, I will call on White Spirits to bind her and remove her."

"I think there is somethin' you need to know about Jillianna Romanitti, Seelah."

"All right, Jack, what is it?"

"Jillianna Romanitti is a vampire."

For a long moment, Seelah continues to stare up at him. "For some reason, I am not getting that she is evil, and if she is really a vampire, she would not be a good spirit."

"Hell no, she's not a good spirit!" Jack begins to pace back and forth in the room. No good spirit would come into a married man's dreams and try and have sex with him."

"She feels that since you fathered a child with her in a past life, you still belong to her. She is a very determined woman." Seelah becomes quiet, closing her eyes and breathing deeply.

Jack sits down on the side of the bed, watching her but not saying anything.

"She is not a normal vampire. By this I mean, she does not attack people and drink their blood. If someone is willing to allow her to take their blood, she does it in a manner that does not put the person in danger of dying or becoming a vampire themselves."

"What happened between us happened in another life probably hundreds of years ago. So, there should be no reason for her to still be havin' the hots for me."

"Except for the child that you and she had together."

"Any child that I had with her is long dead. So, that won't work for an excuse either. I don't think I need to worry 'bout some two hundred year old kid comin' 'round callin' me daddy for Christ's sake."

"No, you're right. No one could still be alive after that many years. Do you know how old the Romanitti woman is supposed to be?"

"Yeah, she told Donavan and me she was close to two centuries old. I thought she was lyin' until I thought back to how long Chandra had lived on this earth."

"Yes, Chandra was very old. The spirit can do strange things when there is evil involved. And, since it is only the body that dies while the soul lives on, the soul will go on to be reborn into many lives."

"What are you tryin' to say, Seelah?"

I think the reason Jillianna Romanitti is still looking at you as belonging to her is that since your soul lived in the body of her gypsy lover and fathered her child, you and she still have ties to one another."

"As I said, that happened hundreds of years ago. Just because she is still hangin' on to life without dyin' and bein' reborn doesn't mean my soul is. I am Jack Olivier', not some gypsy named Karleto."

"Do you want to know why you and she are still tied in this life?"

"Oh, I can't wait to hear this one. Okay, whip it on me, Seelah. Tell me why Jillianna Romanitti believes in her screwed up mind that we're still an item, even though this all happened hundreds of years ago and the kid we had is long gone."

"That is just it, Jack, the child you fathered with Jillianna Romanitti, is not long gone. Her soul lives on in the body of Regina Hindel."

CHAPTER 20

"Hays," Donavan punched the button on the intercom in his office.

"Yeah, Donavan, I just got a call from a Rayford Seals who asked that you and Jack meet him at the Hindel Mansion."

"Did he say what's going on out there?"

"No. It sounded like he wanted to talk with the two of you about something."

"Guess he couldn't figure out that if he could talk with you on the phone, that he could talk with me on the phone."

"I guess not." The man at the desk chuckles slightly.

"Call him back and let him know we'll meet him out there in about an hour."

"Will do."

Donavan pulls the phone over closer on his desk. As he hears the soft voice of Seelah, he smiles. "Good morning to you, Seelah. Is Jack nearby?"

"Good morning, Donavan. Yes, he is out on the patio. I will get him."

"What's up, Partner?" Jack's voice comes on the line.

"Sounds as though you're in a good mood. I hate to ruin it for you."

"If you're takin' that stance, somethin' tells me the Hindel Mansion's involved."

"Dispatch just got a call that Rayford Seals wants us to meet him out at the mansion; that he wants to talk with us about something."

"Seals can't tell you on the phone what he wants to talk with us about? It would be a hell of a lot easier than our drivin' all the way out there."

"I had the same thought. Anyway, do you want to come into the station or just meet me out there?"

"I'll come into the station, and we can ride out there together," Jack said, smiling over at Seelah as she walks by him.

Seelah stops walking and turns to look at Jack. "Jack, ask Donavan to hold on a moment, please."

"Hold on, Donavan, Seelah wants to say somethin' to me."

"Ask Donavan if he would mind my riding along with the two of you. I have a feeling I can be of some help. I'll see if Barb minds watching Donny for a while."

"Donavan won't mind you comin' with us."

"Okay, then I'll get ready to go."

As she walks away, Jack turns back to his conversation with Donavan. "Donavan, Seelah wants to come with us out to the mansion. She seems to think she can help in some way, so we'll both see you in a few."

***

"This Hindel woman is somewhat of a flake. She won't listen to anything we tell her, and she's going to mess around and get herself and Seals killed."

"Just because she's been raised differently don't make her

a flake," Jack shot back at him.

Donavan leans forward in the seat to look across Seelah. "Sounds as though you've had a change of heart where she's concerned. Did something happen between last night and now that I need to know about? I mean this purely in an investigative sense, Seelah."

Jack remains silent.

"Why don't you share with Donavan what we uncovered earlier, Jack?"

"If you found out something I need to know, then I want to hear it."

"I think Jack has told you about the dreams he has been having about the Romanitti woman. She is not only coming into his dreams, she is leaving her body at night to come to our house."

"That's not good. The woman is a vampire. She could be a danger to both you and Donny."

"I am not afraid of her, Donavan. I can always call on the White Spirits to bind her and take her away. If she is bound while she is out of her physical body, she will be delivered over to the dark side, and her physical body will linger in a coma until her body dies."

"Damn, sounds as though the White Spirits don't mess around."

"They can't take a chance on her doing more evil, Donavan."

"Is she evil? Chandra wasn't evil."

"The woman is comin' into my home and into my dreams, tryin' to make me cheat on my wife. I would call that evil," Jack leaned forward to look at Donavan.

"When you put it that way, I have to agree with you."

Donavan slows down as they approach the gate. "Guess

we won't need to wait for someone to let us in."

Jack opens his car door. "I'll push it the rest of the way open."

"No matter how many times I drive up this lane, I still get a sick feeling in the pit of my stomach," Donavan murmurs as they wait for Jack to get back into the jeep.

"There is so much evil on these grounds. I can't believe the Hindel woman and her groundskeeper even want to live here."

Jack slid into his seat. "Seals is walking towards his cottage."

Donavan parks the jeep in front of the cottage and turns off the key. "I guess we're here. Might as well get out and hear what Seals has to offer.

"Donavan, Jack," he shakes both of their hands, "let's go inside where we can talk." He gives Seelah a curious glance.

"Seals, this is my wife, Seelah. I hope you don't mind that she came with us," Jack told him.

Seelah holds out her hand to him and smiles. "I am glad to meet you, Mr. Seals."

"Nice to meet you, ma'am," he takes her hand in his, "and please, call me Rayford."

Seelah nods as Jack guides her forward and into the cottage.

Seals pours them all a cup of coffee, then takes his own chair at the small table. "I guess you're wonderin' why I didn't tell you what I wanted to say on the phone, but I prefer lookin' at the person I'm talkin' with."

"I hear ya," Jack said. "I'm the same way. You get a sense of truthfulness or out and out BS."

"I'll get right to the point since I know you probably have things to get done today. Regina had a surprise visitor yesterday.

A woman by the name of Romanitti. She said she came to welcome Regina to the parish. She brought flowers and a tray of fruits and exotic cheeses. She made sure Regina knows that she is rich and cultured." He huffed out a disgusted breath.

"How did Regina react to all this giving?" Donavan spoke up.

"She was pleased and excited 'bout meetin' someone here who was, as she put it, her monetary equal."

"Okay, but why did you call us all the way out here? Did something happen that we need to know about?"

"I know this is gonna sound crazy, and I can't put my finger on what has me so upset with that woman. Not to mention her and Regina look so much alike they could be sisters. Right now, they're at the Romanitti house visitin', and it's all I can do, not to go over there and drag Regina back here."

Jack glances at Seals with a pleased look on his face.

"Would it be possible for us to go up to the mansion?" Seelah asked, looking from one to the other of the men seated at the table. "I would like to see if the blessing the priest did on the mansion was able to release all of the ghosts trapped there and if not, then maybe I can."

Jack caught the look Seals gives to Seelah.

"My wife's a psychic, Rayford. If she can send any of the souls still trapped there on to the other side, it would be one more protection for you and Regina."

"I have no problem with you wantin' to help. After what went on with the delivery man, I'm ready for any and all help that's offered." Rayford threw up his hands in a posture of surrender.

Jack walks through the door of the mansion first, keeping Seelah's small hand in his as he looks around.

"The priest can be glad. The atmosphere here is a lot more inviting. It is even less heavy than when I sent the child, Jonathan kept here, over to the other side."

"Why would he keep a child imprisoned here? Especially a spirit? What possible good could she do?"

"Jonathan Hindel was a very evil man. All the Hindels were evil. They preyed on the children of this parish. They fed on the bodies of innocent children." Seelah shuddered.

"All right, since I was not here in the parish to see what all went on, I can't argue with you on what you know to be true. But, I can tell you right now, Regina Hindel is not evil. She's a pain in the ass, but she ain't evil."

"Sounds like you're takin' quite a shine to your boss lady, Rayford." Jack grins over at him.

"There's no need to remind me of my position here. I already know this. Regina's made it clear that there won't be anythin' more to our relationship. All I'm sayin' is, for all the bravado she likes to show people underneath it all, she's just a gullible little girl who needs protection. That's where I come into the picture."

The look he shared with the two men watching him left no doubt in their mind, he meant what he said.

Seelah ignored the conversations going on around her to move through the house and into different rooms until she comes to a door that leads off from a den. She opens the door only to slam it shut quickly as a feeling of extreme danger surrounds her.

Jack runs up to her, taking her by her shoulders to gently shake her. "What are you doin' in here by yourself? You know better'n to take off like this."

Seelah leans into his arms, putting her own arms around his waist and hugging him to her.

"What's wrong?" he asked.

She steps back to turn the knob on the door she had just slammed shut. "When I opened this door, I immediately had a feeling of dark evil surround me."

Jack moves her back out of the way to open the door himself. When he flips a switch just inside the door, he can see a set of stairs leading down into a basement.

"Well, what do we have here, folks? Could it be we have found the elusive basement?"

"Are you serious, Jack?" Donavan moves forward to look down the stairs.

"So you found a basement. Most houses have a basement. What's so different 'bout this one?" Rayford looks at them.

"True, except how many do you know of that has been used for human sacrifice and Satanistic Rituals?" Donavan's tone is sharp as he unsnaps his holster, drawing forth his .44 Magnum, before walking down the stairs.

"Are you fuckin' kiddin' me?!" Rayford bellows, then glancing over at Seelah, he murmurs, "Sorry, Seelah, I forget myself sometimes."

Seelah nods as she followed Jack and Donavan down the stairs and into the open basement.

"I'm not lookin' forward to tellin' Regina 'bout this. Not that she would believe me anyway. But this puts a whole nother spin on this evil pile of boards."

"If she won't believe you, then drag her down these stairs and prove it to her," Donavan told him.

"Oh, she'll believe there's a basement down here. She just won't believe what you are sayin' it's been used for."

Seelah moves around the large room, running her hands over the walls, then up to a large and thick plate of white stone attached to tall stone legs painted black.

"What the hell," Jack breaths as he moves forward to pull Seelah across the room.

Everyone stops to stand side by side to stare at a large altar.

"Nothing's changed!" Donavan screams out his anger. "How many times does this pile of shit have to be torn down? No more!" Donavan fires his weapon at the stone altar, again and again, the bullets making pinging sounds as they fly off to the side until finally, all they hear is the click of an empty Magnum.

Jack grabs Donavan around his shoulders in a tight grip. "I gotcha, partner! I gotcha. The hell you and your family went through before is over."

"What the hell did you do that for?" Rayford looks over at the two men standing nearby. "This is all I need." He spins around, staring upward. "Stuff bein' destroyed in Regina's house."

"Are you blind, Seals? Can't you see what the hell you're lookin' at here?"

"Yeah, I can see what I'm lookin' at. It looks like a stage of some sort."

"Stage my ass!" Jack moves forward. "You're lookin' at a goddamn altar! An altar where little kids are sacrificed to the dark side. Donavan's own daughter was almost killed on an altar just like this in the original mansion that stood on these grounds until Donavan and I had it blown to hell!"

"Oh, Christ! And now we see an altar in this house." Rayford looks around. "I gotta get Regina and myself outta this place."

"Jack, the girl who was found on this estate was not sacrificed on this altar. She was killed on the grounds. She was supposed to have been sacrificed, but her sacrifice and the sacrifice of the other young girls who were here was postponed due to the arrival of Regina and Rayford."

"Seelah, you said their sacrifice has been postponed," Donavan said, coming forward. "So this means that there will still be young girls murdered on this estate. Can you see if anyone has already been killed on this altar?"

"No blood has been shed on this altar. But, to answer your question, Donavan, if the altar is not destroyed, there will be blood spilled here."

"We need to get it blown up and fast," Donavan said, keying the mike on his handheld radio.

"Hold on just a damn minute. I can't give you the go-ahead on anything that concerns what happens here. Regina's the owner of this place. It'll have to be up to her what happens."

"Then you best get her ass back here. Because as long as this altar's in place, she runs the risk of wakin' up to the screams of tortured children in her basement and ghouls runnin' 'round her house."

"Jack is right, Rayford. I am sure since, as you said, Regina is not evil, she will see the wisdom in having the altar removed." Seelah places a hand on his arm.

CHAPTER 20

Regina could not stop looking at all the wealth surrounding her. And now that she had found someone who could keep her entertained on the intellectual level befitting her station in life, she knew she could begin enjoying life in the parish.

"I can tell by the happy smile, spreading across your face, that you approve of my home, Regina."

"Oh yes. You will need to share the name of your interior designer with me. Although the mansion is already filled with expensive art and beautiful furnishings, I still want to make the mansion my own, with my own touch."

"I will be glad to help you. After all, what are friends for? And make no mistake, Regina, you and I are going to be very close friends."

"When I think of all the unfair bias directed at me just because my name is Hindel, I want to cry. I am not an evil person, and I never will be. And as far as the people in this parish believing in monsters who murder little children, that is just out and out silly make-believe."

For a long moment, Jillianna remained standing and

staring at Regina, then, taking a deep breath, she decided on her words.

"Regina, there are some things in this world of ours that most refuse to believe they can actually exist. I think the parish stories of the Rougarou is one of those."

Regina laughs aloud, thinking her newfound friend is making a joke. But when she sees the look on Jillianna's face, her voice takes on a more serious tone. "This is the second time you have alluded to the possibility of a monster running loose in the parish as being real. Please tell me you are not serious."

"As someone who has lived on this earth a lot longer than you, I have seen things that a normal person would have a hard time believing in."

"Such as?" Regina's voice is very quiet now and taking on a slight edge of unease.

"Come on, let's go out on the patio and enjoy a glass of iced tea in the beautiful sunshine." Jillianna moves forward to pull Regina towards the patio door. "We are having too good a time to let silliness and superstitions ruin our day."

"All right." Regina allows herself to be pulled along. "I was beginning to wonder if I had made a mistake in allowing myself to become friends with a woman who has the same mindset as the rest of the people in this parish.

"You can put your mind at ease, my new friend. You will never see the day when I take up the beliefs of the close-minded people of Saint Anthony Parish."

Stretched out on one of the lounge chairs, Regina watches Jiallianna laugh and joke with the man who served their drinks and a small plate of chips and dip.

As the man removes himself, Regina declares.

"Do you think it is wise to become so close with the hired

help? I could never do that. I believe they need to know their place, and if we allow ourselves to become friends with them as though they are our equal, it gives them a false sense of worthiness."

"Baxter and I are very close. He has been with me for more years than I care to count. He sees to my needs, and he knows each and every one of my preferences in the men or women I take to my bed when my body is in need."

Regina sits forward in her chair. "You send your servant to pick up a prostitute for you? And, too, aren't you afraid of contracting Aids?"

"Baxter knows he is to find only the cleanest and most alluring. He would never pick up a man or woman off the street. He would only hire someone from a house who makes sure their people are checked weekly to be sure they are free of any diseases."

Regina could only stare over at her.

"I see I am shocking you." Jillianna laughs.

"I have never met anyone like you. You laugh and joke with your servant, and you openly admit to paying someone to have sex with you."

"As I said, Baxter and I have been together for a long time. And I see nothing wrong with satisfying my body's needs. I doubt I could ever be with the same person for any length of time, so marriage is out of the question. This way, I have the best of both worlds. A different lover each week with no strings attached."

"But—how—," she stammers, in trying to form her question.

"How can I have sex with a female?"

"Yes," Regina whispers, her face turning red with her unease in discussing such a personal subject.

"Have you ever been with a female, Regina?"

"No. I have no desire to be with a woman. The thought makes me ill."

"That is your choice, and I hope my telling you of the intimate details of my personal life will not ruin our friendship."

"As long as you don't expect me to be a part of that intimate life, we will be fine." Regina takes a long swallow of her drink.

"Fair enough." Jillianna looks over at her and smiles. "But there is one more thing I would like to know."

"And that is?"

"Your groundskeeper. Is he only your hired help, or is he something more, and is he up for grabs if someone wants to get to know him on a — let's say — more personal level?"

The angry look crossing Regina's face is all the answer Jillianna needs.

Regina reaches into her purse to remove her cell phone as it continues to ring. "Hello."

"Who is it, Rayford?" Regina's tone is surly as she continues to listen to what is being said on the other line. "Oh, for Pete's sake, Rayford, I am not running back to the estate just because they think they've found something that needs my attention."

With that said, Regina shuts off her cell to put it back into her purse.

"I didn't mean to eavesdrop on your conversation, but I couldn't help overhearing that you are needed back at the mansion."

"Yes, Rayford said that Detectives Hays and Olivier' and Olivier's wife are there, and they found something that I need to see."

"It is none of my business, but perhaps since there was a murder on your estate, you should go home. If you like, I will be glad to go with you."

"If you really think I should, then I guess I will. And yes, please come back with me. For some reason, the idea of having you there makes me feel better."

Jillianna smiles and gets to her feet.

CHAPTER 21

"Regina's not up for comin' back right now. She thinks we are all bein' silly. She hung up on me, so I doubt she'll be returnin' any time soon."

"If that's the case, this'll give us enough time to get someone out here with a jackhammer to make short work of this altar," Jack says, pulling his cell from the sheath he has attached to his belt.

"I'm still not ready to destroy property on this estate without Regina givin' the okay. I sure as hell can't afford to pay for any damage."

"Rayford," Donavan steps forward, "this altar puts the two of you in more danger than you already are, just by being here. Don't you care about the fact that kids are going to be murdered right here in this basement? And another thing you need to think about, do you really think they will allow the two of you to live when they know you are in the house and can tell the police what you heard or maybe saw?"

"I see your point, goddamnit, but it ain't you who'll get fired and thrown into the street."

"Would you rather your ass land in the morgue, or at least what would be left of you? By the time the Rougarous are done gnawin' on ya, there ain't much to haul off."

"Okay, give me her number and let me call and talk with her." Donavan holds out his hand.

"It won't do a damn bit of good for you to call her. If she don't want to do something, then you might as well hang it up."

"Donavan, can you find out who the other children are who were on the estate when the one girl was killed? I am sure they are the ones who are being targeted for the sacrifices. If we could warn them off, that would certainly help," Seelah says.

"The department doesn't have their names, but I bet we can find out who they are by going to the school and asking around about who her friends were."

"Rayford." Regina's voice calls out in another part of the house.

"Regina must have had a change of heart." He runs to the stairs.

"Good, now we should be able to get this show on the road since the Queen Bee's arrived," Jack grins over at Seelah and Donavan.

When all three come down the stairs, Jack feels his stomach tighten uncomfortably as he sees the face of Jillianna Romanitti smiling over at him.

"What the hell are you doin' here, Jillianna? We got enough problems without you addin' more."

"Jillianna is my friend, and since this is my estate, I will be the one who says who can and cannot come here." Regina glares over at Jack.

"Yeah, well—," Jack begins, only to halt what he was going to say as Seelah puts a hand on his arm.

"Alright, what is so important that my undivided attention is needed?"

"Do you have any idea what this is?" Donavan walks over to stand beside the altar.

"A stage so we can have live entertainment at our parties?" Regina scoffs.

"No, Regina, what you are looking at here is an altar," Jillianna whispers as she puts an arm around Regina's waist. "Why would an altar be in your basement, Regina?"

"Exactly." Donavan notices the protective way Jillianna treats Regina.

"Regina didn't know 'bout the altar in her basement. Neither did I until Seelah found the stairs leading down here."

"And who are you?" Regina gives Seelah her full attention. The tone of her voice showing her distrust of having a stranger in her home.

"I told you on the phone, Regina, that Seelah is Detective Olivier's wife. She is also a psychic," Rayford hastens to tell her.

"Now I am beginning to see why you felt I needed to interrupt my afternoon with a bunch of voodoo nonsense."

Jack walks forward to pull Seelah close to him. "I know this is your house, Regina, but you would do well to keep a respectful tone in your voice when addressin' my wife." The no-nonsense look on his face telling her he meant business. "If it weren't for Seelah findin' this basement and what's in it, you might have woke up to find one of your bloodthirsty relatives suckin' on your neck."

"You need to listen to him, Regina. Finding an altar in your basement is not good," Jillianna whispers.

"The detectives want to destroy the altar so no sacrifices can be held here. And before you get all bent out of shape, I tend to agree with them," Rayford tells her, his eyes narrowing as he sees the way Jillianna holds Regina close to her.

"And just how do you purpose to destroy a rock altar?"

"With a few nice big sledgehammers, Regina." Jack smiles over at her.

"All right. If you think it is necessary, then, yes, you can destroy the altar."

"I think you have made a wise decision, Regina. Now, do you want to come back to my place or stay here to make sure that nothing else will be destroyed except that which you have given them permission to remove?"

"I think I better stay here. Since you followed me here in your car, this will not present a problem."

Jillianna hugs Regina close as she nods to the others in the room. When her eyes fall on Jack, she smiles. "Have a good day, Detective Olivier' and a good night."

"My husband always enjoys his nights in my arms, Ms. Romanitti. I make sure of it," Seelah purrs as she looks into the eyes of a surprised Jack.

For a long moment, Jack continues to smile down at his petit and spirited wife, then focuses his gaze across the room. "I hope you're not plannin' on gettin' too close to this woman, Regina. If you are, you might find you've escaped the clutches of one ghoul only to be taken in by another one." Jack looks directly at Jillianna as he delivers his warning.

"I will not have a guest in my home disrespected, Detective Olivier', so you will kindly keep your remarks to yourself. Regina's beautiful eyes are hostile as she stares directly at Jack.

"No, it is all right, Regina." Jillianna hurriedly speaks up. "I, like you, am not a popular addition to the parish. I do need to be going, though. Call me?"

"Of course," Regina hugs Jillianna, then steps back to walk up the stairs.

"Am I wrong, Jack, or do you know this Romanitti woman?" Rayford speaks up.

"As a matter of fact, I have had a few run-ins with her." He glances furtively down at Seelah.

"Just like Regina, she's quite a looker, but there's somethin' I don't trust 'bout her. She makes me want to watch my back," Rayford whispers.

"You'd do better to keep a close eye on your throat," Donavan clamps a hand on his shoulder.

Instinctively, Rayford brings a hand up to his throat. "Why, is she one of those broads who like to leave hickies on the neck to show the world she's been there?"

"No, more like she's into havin' her Bloody Mary served warm and without the added veggies."

"I guess I'm slow, but I'm not followin' you." Rayford looks around the room.

"Then I'll spell it out for you, Rayford," Jack tells him. "Jillianna Romanitti's a vampire."

"How dare you say such a wicked thing about my friend." Regina stands on the last step, one hand raised as she points at Jack. "It isn't enough for you to make up filthy lies about my relatives. Now you have to cast aspersions on my friend."

"Ms. Hindel," Donavan walks over to stand in front of her, "you can believe what you want, but the truth is still the truth. Jillianna Romanitti has admitted to being a vampire."

"Get out! Do you hear me? Get out of my house! And you are not to destroy anything in this house! The altar will remain where it is. All you want to do is make up stories about good people!"

Rayford moves quickly across the room and pulls her into his arms. "Regina, you have to listen to these people."

Regina shoves herself away from him. "Don't you dare touch me, Rayford Seals. You know as well as I do there is no such thing as a vampire!"

"Ms. Hindel," Seelah enters into the conversation, "no one wanted to believe that something only seen in movies could exist, but they do. This parish has seen more than its share of evil. I know you are new here and have been raised to believe that evil is only in the psyches of those with unhealthy minds, but please listen. Your very life and the life of Mr. Seals depends on it."

"Get these people out of my house, Rayford. Now!" She turns and runs up the stairs.

"If I had a stick of dynamite, I'd turn this fuckin' altar into powder. We all know if it's left standin', it's gonna be covered in the blood of little kids. And it will be all Regina Hindel's fault."

"I guess we need to leave. This is her estate, and since we don't have a warrant, giving us the right to destroy something we know later on down the road is going to be another crime scene, our hands are tied."

"Yes, Donavan," Seelah places a hand on his shoulder. There will be another murder taking place here. You spoke earlier about going to the school to find out who the friends are of the girl who was already killed on this estate. I think you should go today. Because, if you wait until tomorrow, you may be too late to save their lives."

CHAPTER 22

"I cannot believe how you feed into all this make-believe parish folklore!"

"Maybe you should calm down and listen to what other people, people who just might know what the hell they are talkin' `bout, have to say to you."

"Rayford, are you that much of a silly goose as to believe someone can be a vampire?"

"Maybe." He hunches his shoulders. "I never would have believed there are actual Rougarous either. But, when you see these things with your own eyes, you have to step back and start to think maybe people ain't as crazy as you think."

"And maybe I should be leery of the one I have living on my estate instead of the ones who might break into my house and try and kill me."

"Are you sayin' you want me out of here?" Rayford looked her square in her eyes. "Because if you are, I'm gone. And you can stick this whole goddamn place straight up your ass!"

"I didn't say I want you to leave. I just want you to start thinking about all the crazy things we are hearing and use common sense."

"Look, I don't know if the woman you call your friend is a vampire or just someone who gets her rocks off by tellin' people she is. But, I do know there are monsters roamin' the grounds of this estate and I for one do not feel safe stayin' here. Now we learn, there's a goddamn altar in the basement, and you won't give the okay to have it removed just because you're pissed at bein' told that your new friend's a vampire!"

"If you don't feel safe staying here, then you are free to leave. I will write you a check right now, and you can go find a place that is not threatening."

"And what—leave you here by yourself in this fuckin' mausoleum?" He laughs outright. "Not on your life, Baby. You might be a pain in the ass, but I'm not 'bout to walk off and let whatever is walkin' these grounds turn you into their midnight snack."

"You do what you feel you must. I am going to go over and talk with Jillianna about what I have learned." She grabs up her purse and keys from off the island in the kitchen.

"I don't think that's a good idea, Regina. Even if she isn't a vampire, her tellin' people that she is makes her a nut case. I think you should stay here where I can keep an eye on you."

"Are you telling me you refuse to allow me to leave here?" Regina backs away.

"Yeah, I am. You're gonna put yourself in needless danger, and I'm not gonna allow you to do that."

"Get out of my way, Rayford or you will find yourself out of a job." She tries to walk around him, but Rayford reaches out and grabs her up against him.

"If you're gonna act like a spoiled brat, then that's just how I'm gonna treat you."

Rayford lifts Regina off her feet and throws her over his shoulder to walk into the front room, where he drops her down on the long couch.

Regina tries to scramble to her feet but instead finds herself being thrown, non-too gently, over Rayford's lap.

"What are you doing?" Regina screams.

"What your daddy should of done years ago. With that said, he brings his hand down again and again on her round bottom.

"I will have you arrested for assault!"

"And you can probably make it stick since your little ass should be pretty red by now." He sets her upright on the couch. Then, getting to his feet, he stands staring down at her.

Regina turns onto her side and props her head on the arm of the couch. "No matter what I did, no one has laid a hand on me in all the years I've been alive," she whispers.

"That's plain to see. You're a spoiled brat who thinks only of herself and fuck everyone else. You put others in danger with your narrowed thinkin', Regina, but now you're also puttin' your own life in danger, and I can't allow that. I think too much of you."

"I can't have a relationship with you, Rayford. I have already told you this."

"Yeah, I'm not up to your monetary equal." The tone of his voice is strong and, at the same time, more than a little bitter. "This is true, but here's somethin' I want you to know and remember." He walked over to the couch to lift her into his arms. Without a word, he brings her full mouth up to his. "I may not be rich and successful, but I guarantee you, there ain't another man walkin' who will care 'bout you more than me. His mouth covers hers in a long, passion-filled kiss. When finally he releases her, they are both shaken. "I'm gonna ask you this one time. Do you want me to stay with you tonight? Not just to protect you which I will with all my bein', but do you want me to still be beside you when you wake up in the morning?"

Slipping her arms around his neck, she pulls his mouth back down to cover hers.

"I'll take that as a yes, I want you, Rayford." His voice is deep with emotion.

Without another word, he holds her close in his arms to carry her upstairs to her room. With deliberate slowness, he pulls the loose-fitting dress she is wearing up and over her head.

Regina undoes the clasp in the front of the black lace bra she is wearing to drop it to the floor. When she reaches down to remove the matching panties, Rayford stays her hands.

"Let me," he whispers, pulling down her panties and leaning forward to place a warm kiss on her ash-blond hair before dropping the panties atop the discarded bra.

Rayford picks her up in his arms to lay her gently in the middle of the bed.

He watches her as he unbuttons his shirt one button at a time, then pulls it from his well-toned and muscular body. Slowly, he unzips his tight jeans to shove them down and off his hips before kicking them off to the side.

Without taking her eyes from his, Regina gets off the bed to walk over to him. Without a word, she removes the last remaining piece of clothing hiding him from her hungry eyes.

Turning her to face him, he murmurs quietly, "Do you want this, Regina? Do you want me to make you a woman? My woman?"

"Yes, Rayford," she breathes her words. "Please, make me your woman." She rubs herself roughly against him, fisting a handful of his dark hair to yank his hot mouth down to hers.

He allows himself the pleasure of her caressing tongue before moving his mouth over her throat to the pulsating beat telling him of her arousal.

Rayford looks at her wanting to see his own need mirrored in her dark eyes. He is not disappointed as he moves to capture one aroused nipple in his mouth to suckle it eliciting a soft moan from her throat.

Breathing deeply, Rayford picks her up in his arms to lay her on the bed. Straddling her body, he moves his mouth down over her skin, nuzzling the thick blond hair between her thighs and enjoying the woman smell of her. His searching tongue moves to taste her sweetness, evoking a breathless scream from Regina as she gyrates her slender hips until Rayford quiets her movements, unwilling to miss a drop of her sweet nectar.

Rising up, he looks at her. "Do you want me to stop, Regina? Or do you want me to bring your hungry body the fulfillment it so desires?" His voice sounds rough in his need for her.

"No! Don't stop, Rayford! I want you to end this pain you've awakened in my body. Now!" She pounds her small fists on his naked back.

Rayford moves forward, parting her thighs with his long legs and with a sharp flick of his hips, he enters where no man has been before.

Regina screams as his hard member breaks through the protective shield. She begins to buck, trying to remove him from assaulting her body. Instead of stopping, Rayford moves his rock-hard shaft ever deeper inside her velvet-soft vault until, against her will, she joins him. Moving her body to match his in a desperate need to end this torment until she, at last, screams her surrender.

Rayford throws back his head as he feels the hot juices shoot from his body to slam against the slick walls of her womanhood.

He removes himself and rolls off her body to lie beside her. "I apologize for your pain, Regina. There is always pain when a woman makes love for the first time."

"It was well worth the pain." She smiles over at him.

"I agree. You are a very beautiful woman, Regina. I won't pretend that it doesn't do my male ego a world of good to know I am the first man to touch you." He places a kiss in the palm of her small hand.

To his surprise, Regina grabs his hand to bring it to her mouth. "Please promise me you will never leave. Everyone I have ever loved has always walked away. I don't want that to happen with you."

Rayford gathers her into his arms, kissing the side of her tear-stained face. "You can put your mind at ease, my beautiful Regina. As long as you want me beside you, I'll be here."

CHAPTER 23

Seelah's beautiful face stays in the forefront of Jillianna's mind. Making the red hot anger in knowing Jack belongs to someone else grow ever stronger until she knows what she has to do.

Leaving her chair, she walks inside the house, unable to enjoy, any longer, the many fragrances from her gardens, floating on the night winds.

Seating herself on the couch, she relaxes her mind until she feels her spirit lift from her body, enabling her to travel, unhindered, through the night until she comes to the small house at the end of the block.

"I will not allow you to keep us apart, my Karleto," she whispers, moving into the house and into Jack and Seelah's bedroom.

She stands for a long moment gazing at the small woman sleeping peacefully in the arms of the man she craves.

"This man you call yours belongs to another. Soon you will see this. Soon he will leave your side to come to me where he belongs."

To Jillianna's surprise, Seelah sits up in the bed. "I know you are here, Jillianna. You will follow me from this room where my husband will continue to sleep unharmed and untouched by you."

Seelah slides her long legs off the bed to get to her feet. Without bothering with a robe to cover the long nightgown she is wearing, she walks out of the room and down the hall to the front room.

"You will sit here near me on the couch where we will talk. If you try and do Jack, our son, or me, any harm, I will call on the White Spirits to bind you and take you to the dark side. You do not want this, Jillianna."

Jillianna's spirit materializes, allowing Seelah to see her sitting beside her.

"You are psychic. Alright, but do you really think you are strong enough to go against me? I have lived on this plane for two hundred years."

"And I understand you are also a vampire." Seelah breathes deeply, keeping herself calm.

"Yes, this is true, so you would do well not to anger me, or you could be forced to live out your life as one who lives off the blood of others."

"Jillianna, as a psychic, I have the ability to tell if a person is evil or good. I do not feel you are an evil person, Jillianna."

"Are you aware that Jack fathered a child with me?"

"I know Jack's soul lived in the body of a man called Karleto who was the father of your child. But that was another time. Jack is a completely different man in this life. We cannot live in the past, Jillianna. I don't believe God intended man to remember his past lives."

"Are you a strong believer in God, Seelah?"

"Yes, I am very much a strong believer in our Holy Father. Are you a believer in God, Jiallianna?"

"At one time, I was a believer." Her voice has lost a good part of its bravado. "Now, I am no longer able to walk into a church or touch the hand of a man of God."

"Have you tried to walk into a church or talk with a man of God?"

"I don't dare. I am unclean."

"Jillianna, if there is one thing I have learned in this life it is, that it is never too late to turn your face back to God."

"It is for me."

"Why do you say this?"

"Because I am a vampire!" Her voice rises with her frustration. "Even though it has been many years since I have taken the lives of others to keep my own self alive, I am still guilty of ending lives. And, I am still unable to touch or be touched by a man of God or anything representing God's holy word without sustaining much harm to my person."

Preferring to ignore Jillianna's immediate problems with God and the church, she asks another question. "How do you satisfy your need for blood now?"

"I drink my own blood by making a small cut on my wrist, or if someone is willing to share their blood with me, I indulge their need to live on the edge."

"Do you take the blood from their neck?"

"No, like me, they make a small cut on their wrist for me to drink from."

"And do they become a vampire after they allow you to take their blood?"

Jillianna laughs. "No. This is the new world where anything is possible, even being safe with a vampire."

"Jillianna, I know you have been coming into Jack's dreams and trying to have sex with him. I am not happy about this. No woman who loves her husband wants to share him with another. I understand you want Jack because his soul lived in the body of your lover, Karleto. Jack is not Karleto. You will stop coming into his dreams."

"You said you could call on White Spirits to bind me and take me to the dark side. Would you really do this?"

"Yes, Jillianna, I would and I will if you refuse to heed my warning about staying away from Jack. However, if you will trust me, I believe I can help you."

"You can't help me." She turns away, shaking her head. "No one can help me."

"Will you let me try?"

"I will have to think about this, Seelah. Before I leave, though, I want to say something," she whispers.

"What would you like to say, Jillianna?"

"Thank you. In all the years I have lived on this plane, you are the first human being who has reached out and tried to help me."

Seelah nods, smiling at the spirit of the woman sitting beside her. "Let me know what you decide. In the meantime, I will know if you try to enter into Jack's dreams."

"Jack is very lucky to have a woman who loves him this unselfishly."

Jillianna's spirit disappears into the night.

The sounds of a toilet flushing, then someone moving in her direction, makes Seelah sit back down.

"What's wrong?" Jack spies Seelah sitting in the glow of the small lamp beside the couch as he comes walking, half asleep, down the hall. "You got the middle of the night hungries, too?"

He plops down beside her on the couch.

"We had a visitor."

"I didn't hear the doorbell ring. Who was it?"

"Jillianna Romanitti. She was here to enter into your dream as she has been doing. I brought her out here and warned her what would happen if she did not leave you alone."

Jack jumps to his feet, his tanned face suddenly drained of color. "You were alone with her? She could have attacked you and Donnie."

Jack whirls to move down the hall to check on their son.

"Calm down, Jack," Seelah calls out, stopping him in midstride. "Jillianna is not an evil person. We had a nice talk, and I told her I will try and help her if she will trust me."

Jack retraces his steps to stand staring at her. The angry scowl covering his face tells her to tread lightly. "The woman comes into the dreams of your husband and does everything she can to get him to join her in a sexual romp, and on top of that: she's a goddamn vampire! And here you are talkin' with her like she's some long-lost friend: when what you should be doin' is sendin' her ass to the dark side of hell."

"She needs to be helped, not destroyed."

"And just how do you intend to help a two-hundred-year-old vampire?"

"By taking her to a Catholic Priest for an exorcism."

CHAPTER 24

The full moon shining down on the Hindel Mansion gives the appearance of warm serenity, while up close, the dark energy uncurling from its shadows depicts a far more sinister portrayal.

Rayford and Regina sleep curled up in each other's arms, innocent of what is happening right at that moment in the mansion's basement.

Laid out on the stone altar, a young girl stares up at the inhuman face looking down at her.

"Why are you doing this? You said you love me. You know I will never tell anyone what you are. You know this!" She sobs into the silence.

Her frightened gaze moves to the ones staring at her from across the room: their ugly faces filled with lust and hunger.

Upon seeing a thick knife held in the claw-like hand of the one standing above her, she opens her mouth to scream, only to have her cry for help silenced as the razor-sharp knife is plunged into her heart.

Within moments the altar is surrounded by fur-covered creatures, all snapping and snarling as their sharp fangs rip apart the body of the young girl to feed their ghoulish hunger. The skeletal remains are left to lie on the blood-spattered altar.

The smell of blood is strong in the air, fueling their unsatisfied thirst and hunger for the sweet, thick blood and raw flesh of the innocent.

One of the creatures hears a sound upstairs, telling him they are not alone in the mansion. He moves away from the others to climb his way up the steps.

***

Regina pads, naked, into the bathroom to step into the large shower. She turns a knob allowing a cascade of warm water to flow over her. Taking her time, she picks up a bar of her favorite soap filled with coconut oil and rubs the bar over her slender body.

She jumps as she feels strong arms encircling her tiny waist.

"I hope you are going to share these relaxing moments," Rayford murmurs against her throat.

She turns, and holding the soap in one hand, she rubs the wet bar over his body, eliciting a moan of contentment from his throat.

"You know, feeling your hands rubbing lather over my body woke someone who wants to play."

A light giggle is heard as her hand lowers to rub the soap between his strong thighs. "Then perhaps he should stop being shy and come have fun with his newfound playmate." She rubs herself against his aroused need.

He backs her against the beautiful, blue-green and tiled wall and, with a wicked grin, takes her suggestion.

"I don't think I have ever enjoyed a shower more than I have right here in your arms," Regina whispers, closing her eyes on the euphoric feelings Rayford's caressing manhood is having on her innocent senses.

Rayford's movements become more intense as Regina's warm tongue enters to play and tease the inside of his ear.

Black eyes, staring out from the human face covered in short black fur, watch from the open bathroom door. His breath comes faster as he hears the sounds filtering out into the quiet room.

At the same time Rayford's hot juices splash against the tightening muscles drawing him ever deeper, a satisfied scream leaves Regina's throat.

"I dare say, a woman could get used to receiving this kind of attention every day."

Rayford pulls himself free of her snug grasp and allows the warm stream of water to cleanse his moist manhood as he smiles over at her. "Any time you need my attention, all you gotta do is let me know, Regina Hindel, and I will give you all the attention your beautiful body can handle."

Upon hearing the name of the woman enjoying the touch of the man beside her, the creature moves away from the door to retrace his steps back down the stairs and into the basement, where he and the others of his kind leave the room through a small tunnel leading to the outside.

Much later, as the morning light spills into the room, Regina fastens the pink lace bra and reaches for her matching panties.

Rayford stands watching the inviting sight then moves towards her. "Although I would love to stay and play, my love, I better get busy with things needin' to be done."

"Don't you want some breakfast first? It isn't good to go without eating."

"Naw, I'll pick up somethin' in town. I need to get a few things. Without startin' another row after the very enjoyable night we spend together, I need to know if you've given any more thought to the removal of the altar. If you give the okay, I can pick up a jackhammer while I'm in town."

To his surprise, she smiled over at him. "I am going to leave that up to you. If you think it should be removed, then that is what will be done."

"I must say," he draws her against him to drop a quick kiss on the side of her face, "I am liking this new Regina more and more."

"Don't think I will let you get away with everything, Rayford Seals. I am still in control here," she murmurs as she leans into him.

"If I didn't have so much to get done, I would show you how fast I can change your mind."

"Oh! You are so ornery." She laughs

"Why don't you ride into town with me, and we will have breakfast at a nice restaurant?"

"No, that is all right. I thought I would run over and visit with Jillianna for a while today."

The moment the words were out of her mouth, she looked away from him to continue getting dressed.

"Again, I don't want to get off on the wrong foot with us, but I really wish you would stay away from her. If what Seelah said is true, you could be putting yourself in danger."

"I don't believe in all that nonsense. Please, let's simply try and stay in the real world with our thinking."

Knowing anything else he would have to offer would only bring harsh feelings, he turned and walked out of the room.

Regina finished getting dressed, then walked downstairs

and into the kitchen.

She flipped the button on the coffee maker, dropped a few slices of bread into the toaster and gets out the butter and strawberry jam from the refrigerator.

When all was ready, she sat down at the table to enjoy her breakfast.

Thoughts of the night before moved through her mind bringing a hot blush to her face as she recalled how easily Rayford had turned her frigid body into one that could not get enough of the hot feelings his skilled hands and mouth had introduced her to.

What was she thinking to allow a man who was only her hired help to become her lover? What would her relatives think? A woman of her means had a station in life to uphold. She could not behave like white trash. She found she could rationalize in a calmer manner now that she was no longer in his arms. It would be a lot easier to break off the relationship in the beginning rather than wait. But the only way she could do this is for him to leave.

Did she want to live in this house alone without the protection of a strong man to come to her aid if she needed help?

True, she didn't foster the silly beliefs of the people in the parish, but the presence of an altar in her basement tells her that something is not right and that that something would need to be dealt with.

She needed someone to talk with. Someone who would be able to think with a rational mind and help her figure out what she should do. Without warning, the face of her new friend, Jillianna Romanitti, flashes into her mind.

"Yes," she said aloud, "Jillianna seems like a savvy woman who has been with her share of men: if anyone will know what I can do about Rayford, she will."

CHAPTER 25

Rayford walks into the sheriff's office and up to the front desk.

"Can I help you?" the man behind the desk asked.

"Yes," Rayford said. "I need to see Detectives Hays and Olivier'. Are they in their office yet?"

"Yes, sir. Let me get your name, and I'll let them know you're here to see them."

"Rayford Seals and tell them it's urgent." Rayford was already walking towards the door to their office as the man behind the desk announced his presence. He sees the door open, and Donavan stands to the side to usher him inside the room.

"Come in, Seals. Dispatch said it was urgent."

"I talked Regina into our removing the altar. I think we should get on it right away before she has a chance to change her mind."

"I agree," Jack said, getting to his feet.

"Now the question is where can we get our hands on a sturdy enough jackhammer?"

"That's no problem. The Sheriff's Department has

everything we need to destroy anything we need to destroy,"
Donavan delivered.

"How did you finally get her to decide to let us get rid of
the altar?" Jack asked.

"Let's just say I'm a good persuader." Rayford grins.

"Enough said." Donavan sits down in front of the phone
on his desk, anxious to make his call. "Yeah, this is Hays. I need
you to get a couple sturdy jackhammers along with five deputies
and a dog and meet Olivier' and me out at the Hindel Mansion.
We're leaving right now."

Jack pulls the seat belt into place as Donavan backs out of
the parking space to follow behind Rayford.

"Why did you want a K9 brought out there again?"

"I think there's a good chance that there's another way
into that basement. I'm going to have the deputy and his dog
check all around that place. Do you want to lay some money on
him not finding another entrance?"

"You serious? Nothin' would surprise me 'bout that
gilded pile of shit!"

"I wonder if the day will ever come when we can blow
that fucking place off its foundation, and it will stay gone?"

"That would be nice. But, I don't think Regina's gonna let
it go."

"Answer me something if you will."

"What?"

"I've seen a change come over you where the Hindel
woman is concerned. You want to tell me I'm wrong?"

"Seelah told me that the soul of the child I fathered with
Jillianna Romanitti now lives in Regina Hindel. Hell, they're the
mirror image of each other, and we've both seen what Seelah can
do so, I believe her."

"Odd as it may sound, so do I."

"And added to that, somethin' happened last night I'm not happy 'bout."

"What happened?"

"Jillianna Romanitti paid a visit to our house last night with all intentions of gettin' me to have a romp with her. But instead of gettin' me, she got Seelah who told her, either she knocks off comin' into my dreams to have sex, or Seelah would call on the white spirits to bind her and take her to the dark side."

"That should have put the fear of Seelah in her. How did she take that little choice?"

"I guess she had to agree, except that ain't all. After she was warned off me, her and Seelah sat around havin' a nice little chat."

"Like Seelah did with Paul after he was attacked."

"Yeah, pretty much. So now Seelah thinks she can help Jillianna to stop bein' a vampire."

"How the hell does she intend to do that? The woman says she's been a vampire for almost two hundred years!"

"Seelah intends to take her to a priest for an exorcism."

"Oh, Christ!" Donavan laughs outright. "If she calls Father Green to do it, he's going to wish he never met any of this crew. First, we have him go to the Hindel Mansion to do a blessing to get rid of ghosts and Rougarous, and now he may be called upon to exorcise a vampire."

They watched as Rayford unlocked the gate, pushing it all the way open for them to drive through and up to the house.

"I think we'll wait for the deputies to get here before going down to the basement," Donavan says, getting out of the jeep.

"Don't look like Regina's home."

"She said earlier she was gonna pay Jillianna a visit. I

tried talkin' her out of it, but I might as well of been talkin' to the wind."

"You like Regina, don't ya?"

"I hope we're not gonna start this shit up again 'bout my knowin' my place." Rayford looks him square in the eyes. "For your information, Jack, it just so happens that Regina and me had a meetin' of the minds last night. And we'll leave it at that."

"Sounds fair enough to me," Jack grins.

"Guess we're about to get this show on the road. Here comes backup. I hope two jackhammers will be enough to get the job done."

"It should be," Rayford unlocks the front door.

"I'll wait here for the crew," Donavan said. "I want to get the dog started on the outside."

"I think he'd do better startin' in the basement, Donavan. If there's another way into this place, and we can bet there is, he'll be able to work his way out."

"I want him to check the inside, the outside, and anywhere else we need to know about, Jack."

Rayford looks at Jack as he withdraws his weapon. "I don't think you're gonna have a use for that, Jack. Regina and I been here all night, and if there was anythin' here, I'm sure one of us would have heard somethin.'" He flicked on the light at the top of the stairs.

"Don't be too sure. I'll tell ya the truth. There ain't much that bothers me, but I couldn't live in this fuckin' house. My dick'd shrivel up 'til I'd be doin' good to take a piss after the sun went down."

"I gotta admit seein' that altar scared the hell outta me. But now that we're gonna get rid of it, I think I'll be okay with livin' here."

"What the hell!" Jack breathes as they make their way into the basement to see the remains of a female sprawled out on the altar.

"Oh no!! No! This wasn't here before. This had to of happened sometime durin' the night! This means Regina'n I slept through a kid gettin' murdered!" Rayford hugs his body, trying to make sense of what he was seeing.

"What's going on, Jack?" Donavan asked, then covers his mouth as he sees what they are looking at. "Oh dear Lord!"

"I'll call Perkins. Needless to say, we can't get the altar removed 'til after all this is checked out. There's so much blood spilled here that it's soaked into the stone."

"Does this mean we're gonna have to vacate the premises again?"

"Rayford, why in the fuck would you want to stay here lookin' at an altar with a dead girl on it? It could just as easily been you and Regina lyin' on that goddamn altar."

"I could lie and say that, yes, you will both have to leave until the investigation into what happened here is over, but we already know what the hell happened here. Rougarous," Donavan told him.

"I need to let Regina know `bout this." He turned towards the stairs. "I'll be upstairs on the phone if you need me."

"Yeah, when Perkins gets here, direct him down to the basement," Donavan tells him.

Rayford nods as he runs up the stairs.

Loud whining and growling could be heard across the basement.

"Sounds like the K9s found somethin'," Jack says, already moving across the floor quickly, followed by Donavan.

Almost hidden from the naked eye, a small round stone

juts outward from the basement wall.

"I think we found where they are getting in and out of the mansion, Lieutenant Hays." The dog's handler speaks up.

"I knew there had to be another way in and out of here," Donavan reaches out and pushes on the stone. Immediately the wall slid to one side with steps leading upward to the outside of the mansion.

"It gives me chills knowin' Regina and Rayford were in this house while all this shit was goin' on."

"Yeah, and their being here begs the question, why weren't they killed, too."

"I think we should leave everything as is for Regina to see when she gets back here. Including the body of the dead girl. Never know. It could just wake her up."

"I doubt it. She'd accuse us of staging it all just to get her outta here."

"Here we are worrin' 'bout her livin' in this pile of shit, and right at this moment, she's visitin' with a goddamn vampire.

CHAPTER 26

"What a beautiful surprise, Regina. My day could not have started out any better than to have a visit from you."

Regina gives the woman holding out her arms to her a big hug. "I am in need of someone to confide in, and you were the first one to come to mind."

"Go on out to the patio. I'll have Baxter bring us something nice and cool to drink along with some coffee. Have you had breakfast?"

"Yes, thank you." Regina sits down on one of the lounge chairs then stretches out comfortably.

"Okay, Baxter will bring us something shortly. Now, what can I help you with?"

To the shock of both of the women, Regina burst into tears.

Jillianna quickly sat down beside her on the lounge chair to take her into her arms. "Whatever is wrong, my sweet one?" Jillianna's voice is low and comforting.

"I had sex with my groundskeeper last night," she sniffed, drawing a hand beneath her nose.

Jillianna hands her one of the napkins Baxter has placed

beside a plate of sweet rolls.

"Thank you, Baxter," Jillianna tells him. "I will serve the coffee."

"Yes, Ms. Jillianna. You call now if you need anything else."

Jillianna waited until Baxter has gone back into the house before saying anything more.

"Regina, I don't mean to make light of your being upset, but I have seen your groundskeeper, and if he is anything at all, he for sure is not someone you should feel bad about having sex with."

"He is my hired help. I am not ghetto trash." She burst into another fit of weeping.

"Of course, you are not ghetto trash. You are simply a young woman who fed her appetite with a handsome man who looks as though he could handle anything she needed him to handle."

Regina wipes her eyes and takes a deep breath. "Then you don't think I should tell him he can no longer be in my employment?"

"Can I ask a very personal question?"

"Of course. Ask whatever you want to ask."

"Was this your first time to have sex with a man?"

Regina nods.

"Now he didn't force you to have sex with him, did he?"

"Oh no. Rayford would never do that. He is a very caring and gentle man. He—" She turns away, her beautiful face flushed with her unease.

"I didn't really think he would. Your Rayford seems to me to be a very caring lover."

"The Hindels would turn up their noses at his being only

my hired help."

I bet the women wouldn't. Jillianna thought to herself. "You have every right to be with the man of your choosing, Regina."

"Rayford wants to remove the altar in the basement. I told him he could. He is very protective of me."

"I am glad to hear this. If any of the rumors being bantered about concerning the Hindel Mansion are true, you need to have a man who has your best interest at heart, close by your side."

"Now, I want to ask you a personal question, Jillianna," Regina whispered.

"Fair enough."

Detective Olivier's wife told us you are a vampire. Why would she say something so unbelievable?"

"Because it is true."

Regina edges her feet off the lounge and slowly stands. "You believe you are a vampire? Why would you think this? Vampires are not real. They are only something a writer would put into a book of horror."

"I want you to sit back down and get comfortable, Regina, so I can tell you what you need to know about me and about you."

"You're beginning to frighten me."

"You have no reason to be afraid, Regina. Believe me, you are the last person I could ever hurt."

"All right, I will listen to what you have to tell me."

"Many years ago, I had the misfortune to fall in love with a man who was a gypsy. His name was Karleto. He was a very handsome man and a great lover."

"Was it because the man was a gypsy that they did not approve of him?"

"Yes. That and my father was a very important man in

Romania. My family and I lived in a castle befitting my father's station in life, and as his daughter, I was very guarded to make sure I would remain chaste. See, Regina, at that time, it was the father's right to choose the man his daughter would marry. She had no say so in the matter."

"I did not realize such rights were still followed in this day and age. That had to be terrible for you," Regina whispered.

"Yes, it was terrible for my father had already promised me to a man of much evil. It was rumored he and his family were Rougarous."

"And you believed the rumors?"

"The rumors were spread by the gypsies, who were a very superstitious people. I did not believe the rumors. I thought them stories to frighten the young into behaving themselves."

I feel so bad for you, Jillianna. I am glad to see you were able to leave the country of your birth and come here, where such beliefs are frowned upon.

"The only problem is, I was not able to leave soon enough. I became pregnant with Karleto's child. We were going to run away, but before we could, Karleto was killed, and I was married off to the man my father had promised me to."

"You had to be terrified knowing you were carrying the child of another man. What did your husband do?"

"My mother and I formed a plan to fool my husband into believing I was a virgin when we were married. This plan was successful for a while, but when the child was born, she had the coloring befitting a gypsy, and I was found out."

Regina covers her mouth. "Oh no. What did your husband do to you?"

"He wanted to kill me and my baby. But we were both saved."

"Thank God."

"No, not God, Regina. The one who saved us was a vampire. My husband thought to make me pay for my sin against him for a lot longer than just one lifetime. I would give my soul to the dark side, and I would allow my child to be taken away, never to see her again."

"How terrible for you both. A child belongs with her mother."

"This is what I believe, too, Regina, that a child belongs with her mother."

"But, why would he think he could make you pay for this wrong-doing for more than one lifetime? He wasn't God."

"A vampire can live for hundreds of years without having to die and be reborn, Regina, just as a Rougarou can." Jillianna stands to walk over to a small pond in the yard.

Regina remains seated, watching her.

"How old do I look to you, Regina?"

"I don't like guessing a woman's age, Jillianna. But, I guess you appear to be in your middle thirties."

Jillianna turns and looks at her. "Would you believe I am almost 200 years old?"

Regina gets slowly to her feet and looks around.

"You do not have to be afraid. I told you I could never hurt you.

"No human can live for hundreds of years, Jiallianna."

"You are right. However, a vampire and a Rougarou can."

"I think I should be going. Rayford will be wondering where I am."

"Before you go, there is one more thing I think you should know, Regina," Jillianna whispers, coming forward.

Unable to move, Regina stands watching her.

"Haven't you noticed the striking similarity between us? We look so much alike we could be mistaken for sisters."

"No, I hadn't noticed. I really must be going, Jillianna."

"The reason for our mirror image of one another is you were the child I was forced to give up all those years ago. You were the child fathered by my gypsy lover instead of the man who was my husband, Rolan Hindel."

The ringing of Regina's cell phone has her moving to pull the phone from her purse. With a shaking hand, she lifts the phone to her mouth. "Yes, hello."

Jillianna watches her, noting the terrified look crossing her face.

"What's wrong, Regina?"

Regina turns off the phone and drops it back in her purse. "That was Rayford. He said a girl's body was found on the altar in the basement."

"That would mean she was murdered while the two of you were in the house," Jillianna's voice is raw with tension.

"I have to leave. There is no need for you to come with me. I will be fine."

Jillianna takes Regina's cold hands in hers. "Please don't let what I have told you about myself keep you away from me. I have waited too long, just to lose you again."

"I will have to think about everything, Jillianna. Right now, I need to go home and be with Rayford and the police officers who are removing the altar."

CHAPTER 27

Seelah rings the doorbell then waits for the woman at the rectory to answer the door.

"Yes, come in, please." A short, stocky lady says, wiping her hands on her apron.

"Thank you. I know I should have called instead of simply dropping in. Is Father Green available?"

"Yes, he is in his office. I will tell him he has a visitor. What is your name?"

"My name is Seelah Olivier'."

"It is nice to meet you, Mrs. Olivier. I am Betty Simpson, the housekeeper here at the rectory. I'll only be a moment."

Seelah can smell the good smells wafting up the hall from what she surmises is the kitchen.

"Won't you come in, Mrs. Olivier'? Father will see you now."

Father Green motioned her to be seated. "I feel bad that I am having a difficult time remembering where I have met you before. Guess old age is galloping forward."

"That's all right. We met when you did a blessing on the

Hindel Mansion. My husband is Detective Jack Olivier'."

The priest's demeanor immediately changes.

"I see." He sat down in his chair. "And what do I owe this visit?"

"My request is a very unusual one. You see, Father, I am a psychic."

"All right, and what does your being a psychic have to do with me?"

"I'm not the problem. I have recently met a woman who needs your help?"

"I think we can help her with just about any kind of intervention she could need. Does she have a drug or an alcohol problem? We have an excellent rehab facility I can let her know about. We also have marriage counseling. I think we have every kind of program she could ask for."

"She needs you to perform an exorcism on her."

Father Green remains still, watching her. Then clearing his throat, he leans forward. "An exorcism on a person will have to be sanctified by the Vatican. This could take a long time."

"She needs an exorcism as soon as possible. She has waited long enough to have a life she can be happy in. She cannot even enter a church."

Are you saying she is demon-possessed?"

"No, she isn't demon-possessed."

"How old is the woman you are wanting to help? Is she old enough to be worried about her mind being impaired with dementia?"

Seelah could feel herself getting irritated with the tone of voice and the lax manner of the man seated across from her.

"Look, Father Green, I know with your being a priest, you have seen and heard things a lot of people think is only make-believe, but this woman needs help. You were able to help with the Hindel Mansion, at least with the getting rid of ghosts and dark entities. The mansion is still infested with Rougarous. Maybe sometime you can find time to get rid of those too. However, right now, I am trying to help a woman who is a two-hundred-year-old vampire. Can you help her?"

"My dear lady!" Father Green gets to his feet to stand staring at her. "I think the one you need to be worried about is yourself! If you believe there are actually living, breathing vampires, I suggest you take yourself to your doctor and tell him what you have told me."

Taking a deep breath to rein in her anger, Seelah tries to use reasoning. "Father Green. When Detective Hays first spoke with you about doing a cleansing on the Hindel Mansion, did you have a problem with his request?"

"Mrs. Olivier', there is a big difference with cleansing a house of those who have left the earthly body God has loaned to them and believing a person can be a Rougarou or a vampire."

"Then you are telling me that you have no problem with believing in ghosts and demons. The problem you have is believing in Rougarous and vampires."

"The creatures you speak of do not exist except in the mind of a person with mental issues."

"Alright, then would you be willing to be a part of a little conspiracy? Since this lady thinks she is unable to enter a church or even touch the hand of a man of the clergy, will you simply do a blessing on her and allow her to believe that she is now clean and able to touch your hand and enter the church?"

"We don't make it a habit of deceiving people." He looks at her sternly.

"I don't make it a habit of deceiving people either, Father

Green, but life is not made up of only black or white. Sometimes the color green is called for."

"What does the color of green have to do with this conversation?"

"The color of green is the color of healing. I will be going now since I can see you are not able to help in this situation. Have a nice day."

Seelah rises to her feet and, without a backward glance, walks out of his office.

CHAPTER 28

As Regina drives to the mansion, she turns over in her mind all that Jillianna told her and also how she feels about what happened between herself and Rayford. She smiles in spite of herself as she thinks on the way she behaved in his arms, admitting to herself that, even now, her body cried out for him.

Driving up to the gate, she is surprised to see Rayford waiting for her.

When she stopped the car, he walked around to get in on the passenger's side.

"I wanted to be alone with you before we get to the mansion so I can hold you and know you are safe."

His caring has Regina holding onto him and meeting his hot mouth with her own.

"I've been worried sick since you left." He propped his chin atop her head, inhaling the sweet fragrance of her coconut oil shampoo, its heady aroma calling to mind their togetherness in the shower.

"I am glad you are here. I didn't want Jillianna to come back with me this time when you told me what was going on with the altar. I feel so safe here in your arms, and I don't care if you are only my hired help. I don't want to be anywhere but here in your strong arms."

"You don't know how good just hearing you say this makes me feel."

A light tap above the car's window has them both turning around.

"I don't mean to break up the party, but we need you up at the mansion." Jack stands grinning at them.

"Jump in the back seat, and we'll get up there," Rayford tells him.

"Good mornin', Ms. Hindel. You look like you're in good spirits this mornin'."

Regina looks in the rearview mirror and smiles.

"I hate to ruin your day, but since this is your property, you're the one who's gonna have to sign off on the removal of the altar and also the body."

Regina brakes the car in front of the front porch.

"Don't worry, I'll be right there with you," Rayford tells her, his voice low with feeling.

"We will all be there beside you." Jack reaches for the door handle then stops. "Ms. Hindel, I need to ask you this. Since we know that this young girl was murdered in your basement while you were in the house, do you still think you should stay livin' on the estate? You never know; the next person to be murdered could be you."

Regina gets out of the car and walks up the sidewalk to the front porch. "Right now, I don't know what I am going to do. I do know that I will not simply walk away from my mansion. I have waited too long to have a house such as this to call my own."

Rayford places his hand on the small of Regina's back as

they walk into the house."

"I'll be right back," she tells Rayford, and then, without thinking, she leans forward and places a quick kiss on the side of his face, ignoring the surprised look Jack is aiming her way.

"I know you have her best interest at heart when you try and get her to give up this evil pile of shit, Jack. I agree with you. And I am not braggin' when I tell you this. Instead, I'm tryin' to ease your mind. I'm gonna be stayin' in the house from now on. Well, as long as she keeps the place."

Jack reached out his hand. "I'm glad to hear this. I know Donavan will be too."

"All right," Regina walks up to them, "I think I am ready to see what we have in the basement."

"Don't bet on it," Jack murmurs under his breath.

The mutilated body of the murdered girl is still in plain view on the altar. Black hair is fanned out around her while bulging eyes mirror the last moments of her life.

Blood no longer drips from the skeletal remains left intact beneath the girl's head but is soaked into the smooth stone, making it appear as though it has been painted a deep, dark red.

Upon seeing Regina standing with Rayford and Jack, Donavan walks over to them. "What you are looking at, Ms. Hindel is a girl who was used in a dark ritual. Her throat, as you can see, has been torn out, and her bodily organs have been eaten. It would be my guess, for some sick reason, that her head was left uneaten so she could be identified, and all this took place while you slept peacefully in your bed upstairs. I guess she didn't get a chance to scream for help, or I am sure you would have heard her."

"All right, Hays, I think you've made your point," Rayford says, a slight warning sounding in his tone as he places a protective arm around Regina's waist to pull her against him.

"Have I made my point, Ms. Hindel? I hope so. Otherwise, this will keep happening." Donavan looks straight over the body to stare at Regina. "I am going to suggest something you may want to have done, Ms. Hindel."

"What is that?" she whispers, still staring at the horrible scene meeting her eyes.

"We found the entrance to and from this basement. If you will come with me, I'll show you what I am talking about."

"Come on, Sweetheart, I am right here with you," Rayford tells her.

Donavan walks to the wall and pushes on the protruding button. Instantly the wall slides to the side showing steps leading to the outside. "This is how they are getting in and out of here."

Regina covers her mouth and shakes her head.

"And to answer your question before you ask it, yes, they knew you were in the house."

"Oh my god, my god, my god," Regina cries, burying her face against Rayford's chest.

"What is it you want to suggest be done, Hays?" Rayford holds Regina against him.

"I would like to suggest this place be blown off its foundation, again, but I am sure that won't happen, so what I will have to be content with is suggesting you have the entrance to and from this basement filled in with concrete, so it is useless."

Donavan turns as a deputy taps him on the shoulder to hand him a sheet of paper for the removal of the altar.

"Ms. Hindel, we're going to need you to sign this piece of paper giving us permission to remove the altar."

"What about getting the girl's body removed?" she asked.

"The cornier will have to sign off on that after we state the crime scene is finished being investigated. Since we already know what happened here, I don't see the need to hold up getting her body removed from the estate."

Donavan hands her the paper along with a pen.

"You are making the right decision in having the altar removed, Regina," Rayford whispers as she scrawls her signature across the bottom of the paper.

"Are we going to have to leave again, Detective Hays?"

"No, as I told Rayford earlier when he posed the same question. Although, I will, again, suggest you get out of this house as soon as possible."

"I think we will be all right since no one will be able to get in or out of this house without our knowing."

"Just make sure you don't answer the door late at night, Jack tells her, then motions Rayford off to the side.

"If you really do have any input with her, then by all fuckin' means, get her the hell outta here."

"I intend to start workin' on it. This place gives me the creeps, and now that we see what is layin' across the room with her throat torn out, it gives me the creeps even more," Rayford tells him quietly.

"Rayford," Regina calls to him, "I want to leave until all this is cleared away."

"I feel the same way. We've done all we can do here, right now, anyway."

"Before you leave, Ms. Hindel, will you give your permission on our having the outside entrance to the basement filled with cement so as to make certain you will be somewhat safer here?" Donavan asked her.

"Yes, do whatever you need to do to secure the estate." She throws up her hands as she walks away.

"Jack, give Phil Lawson at Lawson Ready Mix a call and order up a little over 10-yards of cement. I think that should be enough for what we need done."

CHAPTER 29

Father Green leans back in his chair, thinking on all the woman, who had just stormed out of his office, had to say, and he felt a wave of anger crawl over him.

"We have angry ghosts who refuse to vacate a dwelling they have called their own for years and demons who go out of their way to do the work of Satan, and she wants to add a vampire to the list."

"I'm sorry, were you speaking to me, Father?"

"No, Betty," he said, smiling as she sat a plate of sweet rolls beside a portable coffee pot. "I was thinking aloud about the lady who just left here."

"She seemed like a nice enough person."

"She could be with some mental health intervention." He served himself a sweet roll, poured fresh coffee into his cup. "She wants me to do an exorcism on someone who believes she is a vampire."

"Oh my." Betty brings her hand up to her throat. "That is frightening."

"I feel bad that I was so abrupt concerning her request. Sometimes Satan uses the guise of something completely different than what it really is."

"Do you think this is what could be happening this time?"

"I don't know, maybe. Perhaps I'll give her a call later this evening after I hear confessions."

***

Seelah stretches her legs out on the footstool and picks up the Parish Herald newspaper. "It is getting so I dread looking at the obituaries. I am always afraid of seeing the face of someone I know," she said as Jack sets down in his recliner.

"I hear ya. Now that the Hindels are back doin' what they do best, it's anyone's guess what can happen next."

"I talked with Father Green today while you and Donavan were at the mansion. He seems to feel I could use some mental health counseling." She laughed a slight laugh.

"You can't blame him. How many people would believe a person could be a 200-year-old vampire? Did he throw you out, or did you leave on your own?"

"I left on my own. I did leave in a huff, though, and I am sure he knew I was not happy."

Jack turns in his chair to answer the phone. "Detective Olivier'." He glances over at Seelah with a broad smile. "Yes, Father, she's right here."

Seelah takes the phone from Jack. "This is Seelah Olivier', Father Green. What can I do for you?" Her tone of voice is not unfriendly.

After a few moments, Seelah replies, "Thank you. I will get back with you as soon as I talk with the woman in question. Again, thank you, and I am glad you called Father Green. Until then."

"Sounds like the good father's had a change of heart." Jack glances over at her.

"Yes, he has. He has agreed to meet with Jillianna Romanitti and see what she has to say."

"This should be interesting. And as much as I would love to be present when all this is goin' on, I think I'll let you handle it."

"I get the feeling Father Green has not had a change of heart in believing that she is a vampire or that the Hindel Mansion can be filled with Rougarous. He has had a change of heart about turning someone away whom he feels needs mental health intervention."

"On that note, I agree with him one hundred percent. It's one thing to be a lady of the night, but to believe you are a lady of the night who goes around drinkin' the blood of others to stay alive, is reachin' the limits of sanity." Jack rises to his feet and comes over to where Seelah is sitting. "I still wish you would stay away from her. She ain't one to trifle with or trust."

"I'll be all right, Babe, but thanks for worrying about me." She looks up as he leans over to drop a kiss on her full mouth.

***

Father Green leaves his office and walks across the lawn to the church, suddenly in need of the warmth of God's House. He enters through the back door and moves around the room to kneel in front of the altar. His blue eyes stare up at a large crucifix, feeling, as he always has when seeing the crown of thorns atop the Savior's head, a deep sadness enters his heart.

"I need your help, my blessed Savior. May the blood you have shed for our sins wash away the evil that Satan, in his eagerness to lead Your children astray, has beset upon our parish. Give me the right words to say when a child of our Holy Father comes to me in need. I ask this in Your Holy Name, my Jesus."

On his way back to the Rectory, he sees a man dressed in a dark hoodie and jeans standing off to the side of the church.

"Is there something I can help you with?" He walks over closer to the man watching him.

His only response is a deep guttural growl.

Father Green backs up as the one in front of him lifts his head to show a face covered in short dark hair. "What are you?" he whispers.

"You will stay away from the Hindel Mansion. You are not wanted there. To return will mean your death."

"You are not stronger than God, follower of Satan. Your strength is in fear. I am a man of God! I do not fear you."

"You should. All who blaspheme the name of our father Satan should fear his wrath."

"You will leave here. These grounds surround the house of God. Your evil is not welcome here."

"You have been warned. Your God cannot protect you from the legion of darkness. Only the Master can protect his children."

Father Green backs up until he is standing in the doorway of the church. Reaching behind him, he turns the knob to push open the door.

"Prove your words, evil one! Step inside the walls of God's house and see what will befall you!"

The creature moves forward until it is almost inside the church, then steps back as the priest holds out his hand.

"Take my hand, evil one. Step over the threshold of this dwelling."

Without warning, the creature turns to run from the church.

"Tell all those who have turned their face from the Holy Father who is the strongest on this plane!"

A woman who has been watching from a safe distance

turns and walks quickly back to her car.

Father Green hurries his steps to the Rectory.

Betty steps back as he enters the hallway. "Father, whatever is wrong? You are as white as a bale of cotton."

The priest remains silent as he walks into his office to take a decanter of his favorite whiskey from the small end table beside his desk. Removing the stopper, he pours a hefty amount into a glass.

"Did something happen in the church, Father?"

"No, but only because evil knows it is not strong enough to enter into the house of God."

Father Green sits down at his desk and pulls the phone over close. After placing the numbers he needs into the phone, he waits for someone to pick up on the other line.

"I'll go make some fresh coffee," Betty tells him, already walking away.

"Hello, my name is Father Green. I'm calling to get ahold of Detective Olivier'. I would appreciate it if you would have him give me a call as soon as possible. He already has my number. I would call him myself, but it is late, so I will let you place the call. I will let him know what this is concerning when I talk with him.

***

"My favorite part of the evening," Jack whispers as he pulls Seelah closer against him.

"Mine too, my darling. She leans back and, reaching up, removes the pale pink nightgown keeping her hidden from his hungry eyes.

"I've thought about having you in my arms all day, and now my wait is finally over.

His breath catches as Seelah's warm mouth covers a hard nipple then begins to suckle the small bud.

The shrill ringing of the phone has both of them choosing to ignore its intrusion.

In a quick move, Jack thrusts upward, entering the warm snugness he craves only to realize his rock-hard erection is shrinking to a soft and flaccid memory.

Snatching up the phone, he barks into the receiver. "This had better be fuckin' important."

Within moments he slams the receiver back down to get to his feet.

"What is it, Jack? Is someone in trouble?"

"He sure as hell will be if this ain't as important as he's makin' it out to be. The good father called into the department askin' for them to have me call him ASAP!" He said I already have his number."

"I have the number in my address book. It's by the phone in the kitchen. I'll go get it." She slips her arms through the sleeves of a silk, light blue robe.

After making a quick trip to the bathroom, he calls the number Seelah hands to him.

"Yeah, hello. This is Detective Olivier'. What's so all-fired important that it can't wait until tomorrow?" Jack doesn't bother to hide the anger he is feeling from his voice.

After listening to what is being said on the other line, he becomes more accepting of the need to be involved with what is going on. "Let me give my partner a call and see what he wants to do. I'll be in touch."

Jack hangs up the phone to sit quietly.

"A Rougarou," Seelah whispers.

"Yeah, a Rougarou. It came right up to the entrance to the church."

"What did it want?"

"It was there to warn Father Green to stay away from the Hindel Mansion."

CHAPTER 30

"For a Rougarou to come face to face with a Catholic Priest and threaten him with what will happen if he shows his face at the Hindel Mansion again tells us this parish is in for a lot more murders."

"Yeah, they're makin' it plain they're pissed about losin' the Hindel Mansion as their place of sacrifice."

I have an idea. Since we know that most of the ones who are being sacrificed are young girls, how 'bout we take a ride over to the high school? We can call the principal and have him set up an assembly in the auditorium."

"I think that's a great idea, Jack. We should have already done it by now."

***

"Good morning, everyone. My name is Detective Donavan Hays of the Saint Anthony Parish Sheriff's Department. I am here along with my partner, Detective Jack Oliver' to speak with you on an important matter. The last time we spoke here at the school, it was to warn you about something happening in the parish you needed to be aware of. The reason for our being here today is no different."

Jack looks out over the auditorium at all the young faces staring back at him. "I wish it had not been necessary for your principal to call an assembly today, but I would rather you be a little inconvenienced and safe than to have suffered the fate of your classmate, Jennifer Teals, who was found murdered on the Hindel Estate."

A loud chorus of moans and weeping is heard as the detectives watch to see how the news of the murder of one of their peers is being received.

"Jennifer's parents were doubly shocked to learn that not only had their daughter been murdered, but also to learn she had been murdered on the Hindel Estate when they were of the belief she was safe in her room for the night," Donavan says.

"Are any of you aware of who she was seein'?" Was she seein' someone she didn't want her parents to know 'bout; since they thought she was safe in her bed then come to find out she was out and about. Sounds like she had a late date. If you don't want to say here, you can always call the sheriff's department later. You need not give your name, and if you do, you can feel safe that your name will not be made public," Jack tells them.

"A lot of times, we don't speak up out of fear of being harmed ourselves or being called a narc. But, if you had any feelings for Jennifer, then it is your obligation to come forth with any help you can offer in helping us to find Jennifer's killer."

The principal steps to the podium. "This concludes our assembly. You can all return to your classes. Thank you for coming to listen and maybe to help the Sheriff's Department learn who is responsible for what happened to one of our own students, Jennifer Teal."

***

Jack pulls the seat belt snug across his chest. "So what do you think? Did you get any feelin's on what we can expect 'bout gettin' a hit on who she was seein'?"

"Not really. But you opened the door with what you said about the parents thinking she was snug in her bed while instead, she was out on a late date. That could bring someone forward with at least the name of her date."

"I might see what Seelah can get on who she was with, too. I don't want her to view the body; 'sides, I think she would do better going to where the murder happened."

"No use wasting an in. As always, when dealing with the Hindel cockroaches, we need all the help we can get."

***

"Can't you feel it? It is like a shroud of darkness surrounding this entire area." She stretches her hands wide to encompass the area where the altar had stood.

"This whole damn place gives me the creeps. Always has. But, no, it all feels the same to me," Jack tells her.

"I don't feel anything either, Seelah. The reason you do is because you're psychic." Donavan steps back as he sees spots of blood on the basement floor. "She needs to get this blood cleaned up."

"So, are you gettin' anything we can use or not? If you're not, then I'm ready to get the hell outta this dump."

"The young man she was with was dressed in a dark hoodie and jeans."

"That sounds like the same evil piece of puke who threatened the priest outside the church. The way you describe what he was wearin' fits exactly."

"He tried to get the murdered girl to join him in giving her soul to the dark side. When she refused, they used her in a sacrifice."

"Can you get his name, Seelah?" Donavan comes forward.

"His name is Dick Eldin. He and his entire family are Rougarous. The Eldins have a family-owned business of heavy equipment rentals."

"Too bad we didn't know this ahead of time. We could have used a couple of their jackhammers to take down the altar."

"Yeah, then we could have spread the word about the parish that it was the Eldins who let us use the jackhammers, free of charge, to destroy the altar found in the basement of the Hindel Mansion."

"No reason we still can't."

"Was Dick the one who did the murder, Seelah?"

For a long moment, Seelah remained silent then nodded. "Yes, he is the one who plunged the knife into her heart."

"Thank you, Seelah. Now we have a place to start in getting this murder wrapped up."

***

Donavan and Jack walk through the door of the Eldin business to see a pretty young woman at the desk.

"Hello, can I help you?" The smile she gives them is the real thing.

"I certainly hope so, Cathy," Jack says, peering closely at the name tag pinned above her full breasts."

She laughs aloud at Jack's antics. "How can I be of help to you?"

"We're here to see Dick Eldin. Is he here?"

"Which Dick are you looking for?"

"Oh, I didn't know we had a big Dick and a little Dick." Jack snickers, bringing a bright blush to the young girl's face. "I guess in that case, we'll go with the smaller dick."

The young woman leans forward and flips a button. "Dick, there are two gentlemen here to see you at the front desk."

"I'll be there in a few minutes. Thanks, Cathy," a high-pitched voice replies.

"So tell me, Miss Cathy, have you been with the company long?" Donavan asks.

"No, only a few months. Dick and I are engaged to be married soon."

"Hope she hasn't put a lot of money into the weddin' gown," Jack turns to the side, speaking quietly.

"Yeah, I hear ya." Donavan gives a slight laugh.

"I understand you're here to speak with me? I think I can safely say we have about any type of heavy equipment you could need."

"How about sturdy jackhammers? Do you have those?"

"Yes, we do." He smiles a big grin. "How many do you think you will need?"

"Oh, I don't know. We're going to be taking out a large altar in the Hindel Mansion. What would you say two, maybe three should do the job?"

Both detectives watch the young man closely and are surprised to see the calm way in which he interacts with their mention of the Hindel Mansion and especially plans on the removal of the altar.

"What is the altar made of? Perhaps you can get by with renting only one jackhammer." The look he gives them holds none of the fear they are hoping to see.

"The answer to your question is the altar is made of dyed black, Alabaster Stone."

"Tell me, Dick. Do you know a young girl by the name of Jennifer Teal?"

He turns his head to one side in thought. "No, I can't say as I do. Honey, do you know the girl they are talking about?"

"No, I don't recall anyone by that name."

"Cathy is my fiancée. We are going to be married soon."

"That's odd because your name came up as someone who knew Jennifer."

The expression on the young man's face never changes.

Cathy turns away to wait on a woman who walks up to the desk.

"I think we need to talk in my office. This is the time of day when a lot of people come in."

As they make their way down the narrow aisle, Donavan looks over at Jack.

"Either he is one cool customer who has nothing to fear, or Seelah was seeing the wrong man."

"I'll trip him up. Seelah don't make mistakes, not when it comes to seein' evil."

"Will it bother anyone if I light up?" He pulls a cigarette from a pack lying nearby and sits down at a large desk, motioning the detectives to do the same.

"No, that's fine. In fact, I'll join you," Donavan tells him. Not that I need to calm myself."

"Why would I need to calm myself? You asked if I know a girl by the name of Jennifer something, and I told you I don't."

"Have you ever been to the Hindel Mansion, Dick?" Donavan leans forward in his chair.

"No, I have never had the pleasure." He blows a stream of smoke into the air.

"Lotta strange stories are spread 'bout that place. Some say Satanic Rituals are held there. 'Course, only a brain-dead moron would believe that." Jack gets to his feet. "I mean, get real, for Christ's sake. Who in their right mind would have respect for somethin' God Himself kicked out of heaven?" Jack laughs.

"You never know what to believe anymore. But, getting back to this girl you were asking about, who was it that said I knew her?"

"Hell, I can't remember now."

"I'm sure we'll be able to find out if you did know her. And, if you have ever been to the Hindel Mansion." Donavan and Jack pull their badges from their shirt pockets. "I'm Detective Donavan Hays of the Saint Anthony Parish Sheriff's Department, and this is my partner, Detective Jack Olivier'. We're here investigating the murder of Jennifer Teal."

"You're wasting your time here, Detectives, and I think we have said all we have to say on the matter of Jennifer Teal and the Hindel Mansion."

"Got some advice for ya, Little Dick, if you did have anything to do with the murder of Jennifer Teal, a name I notice is slidin' more easily off your tongue, we will find out. You see, Little Dick, Detective Hays and me have brought down our share of the big bad Rougarous who thought they were invincible. Ask anyone about the Hindels, and they'll tell ya, they're nothin' but a memory."

"Let's go, Jack. Thanks for all your help, Little Dick. Until next time."

CHAPTER 31

Seelah and Jillianna sit quietly in Father Green's office, awaiting the priest.

"I can't believe I am here and actually doing this," Jillianna says.

"You're doing the right thing, just trust me. God will bring you through this."

"Good afternoon, ladies. I apologize for keeping you waiting." Father Green walks around to seat himself behind his desk.

"Thank you for seeing us, Father Green. This lady is my friend, Jillianna Romanitti."

The priest holds out his hand to Jillianna, who merely smiles at him and keeps her hands laced together in her lap."

"Ms. Romanitti, is there a reason you refuse to take my hand in welcome?"

"As I am sure Seelah has told you, and since this is the reason for our being here, I am a vampire and thus unable to touch the hand of a man of the cloth."

"I see." He smiles, shaking his head back and forth. "Let

me ask you, have you ever sought mental help for this affliction you believe you have?"

Jillianna smiles over at him. "No, I have not, since I do not have a mental issue."

"All those who do have mental issues believe themselves to be sane, just as you do."

"All right, since I see no other way to convince you, give me your hand," she tells him, holding her hand outward.

Father Green glances over at Seelah, a broad grin covering his face. "Please pay close attention, Mrs. Olivier'. You are about to see what I have been trying to tell you."

"Oh, I intend to, Father, as I would not miss this for the world."

Jillianna takes the hand of the priest into her own and then releases her grasp as she and the man, whose smugness already has her seething, feel extreme heat covering sweating palms that are quickly covered with angry welts and large blisters.

Seelah grabs both their injured hands to shove them into a pitcher of ice water sitting on the desk.

"You are not a vampire!" Father Green steps back, shaking his wet hand and clutching the cross hanging from his neck. "You are a demon from hell!"

"Enough!" Seelah tells him. "Jillianna Romanitti told you she is a vampire. I told you she is a vampire. This is why we are here. You are a man of God. It is your place to help when one of God's children has been touched by evil."

"I intend to help. I will perform an exorcism to rid this child of Satan's evil."

"This is all we ask. No matter what you are performing an exorcism for, an exorcism is an exorcism and should work to rid one's soul of the curse of a vampire or the curse of a demon."

Betty put salve on their injured hands and wrapped them in gauze. "I hope this helps," she whispers, still shaken by what has happened.

"Thank you for your kindness." Jillianna smiles at her.

"Come with me," Father Green tells them.

"Where are we going?" Jillianna whispers.

"We are going to the church so I can do an exorcism.

"I am unable to enter a church."

"You can at least try. We will ask God to surround you with the White Light of the Holy Spirit to keep you safe."

"Father, are you sure she will be safe? You just saw what happens when she touches the hand of a man of God. You are talking about her entering into the house of God. Can't you perform the exorcism right here in your office?"

Father Green stares over at her. "We will try and enter the church first, and if we can't, then we will do the ritual here."

"I'm so frightened," Jillianna whispers.

"There is no reason to be afraid, Ms. Romanitti. In this day and age, I see a lot of evil. This is almost like it was many years ago."

"Yes, there was much evil then. So much more in Romania than here in America."

"Is this where you were born, in Romania?"

"Yes."

"All right, I am going to go into the church and get everything ready for the exorcism. Do you want to try and step over the threshold?"

"No." she backs away. "I don't dare step foot in the church."

"Then the two of you wait here while I get everything ready, and we will go back to my office."

"Thank you, Father Green," Jillianna whispers, her voice filled with sadness.

"It will be all right." He moves to touch her shoulder then steps back. "You are still a child of God, and He will not forsake you."

As the priest walks into the church, Seelah comes forward. "Jillianna, I am glad you are doing this. The life you have lived thus far on this earth is not one you chose to live."

"I have achieved what I wanted to achieve. I have found the child I was forced to give up. She is a beautiful young woman. And, I am happy to see that my Karleto, whose soul now lives in the body of Jack, is also very happy."

"I am glad you are able to see all this and appreciate how a person, whose soul was unhappy most of the time in a past life, can be very happy in their new life."

"Yes, it seems my life has come full circle."

In Father Green's office, Jillianna stands straight in front of the man dressed in a white robe, and she waits for him to begin.

"In the name of the Father and of the Son and of the Holy Spirit," Father Green intones in a sing-song voice as he sprinkles holy water over the head of Jillianna Romanitti.

To the horror of all those present, the beautiful young woman standing before them begins to age until she falls into a heap of dust beneath the garments that only moments earlier had surrounded the body of a woman who had lived on this plane for almost 200 years.

Father Green steps back, unable to believe what he is seeing. "What is happening?"

"You released the soul of a woman cursed to live on this plane as a vampire, back to our Holy Father. Thank you, Father Green. I knew I could depend on you to make her life better."

"You knew this was going to happen?" His voice is filled with unease.

"I didn't know for sure, but one cannot live on this earth as long as she did and be left whole when released from an almost 200 year old curse."

Seelah smiles as she sees the spirit of Jillianna Romanitti lift from the pile of dust at their feet.

"Thank you, my friend," Jillianna calls out before turning to walk into the light.

"Go with God, Jillianna." Seelah lifts her hand in farewell. "Go with God."

CHAPTER 32

"Glad you could both come over. I waited to call you until we had Donny settled for the night. He certainly doesn't need to hear any of this."

"What's going on, Jack." Donavan takes the drink Seelah hands to him.

"I told you earlier in the week about Seelah talkin' with Father Green about Jillianna bein' a vampire and seein' what could possibly be done to help her."

"Yeah, and I can imagine what he had to say 'bout the whole thing. He still isn't hip to the whole Rougarou belief."

"I'd say he's got a better perspective now that he sees there's a lot more goin' on in the parish than he wanted to know."

"Why do you say that?"

"When Seelah and Jillianna were unable to convince him of the fact Jillianna's a vampire and that she was unable to touch the hand of a man of God, she decided to prove her point by taking hold of his hand. With red welts and large blisters covering the hand she had just touched, he could not deny that something otherworldly was going on, and he agreed to perform an exorcism."

"This is getting downright eerie," Barb murmurers, getting to her feet and walking over to the small portable bar to replenish her drink. "Anyone else need a refill while I'm here?" When they all shook their heads, she walked back to sit down, making sure to sit as close to Donavan as the small love seat would allow.

"I thought an exorcism had to be sanctioned by the Vatican, Jack said."

"That's usually the way of it, but the priest could see the woman who had just given him one hell of a burn with just the touch of her hand, was in dire need of bein' helped right then."

"I certainly hope he was able to help the poor woman." Barb takes a large gulp of her drink.

"I'll let you tell what happened next, Seelah," Jack tells her, dropping a quick kiss on her cheek.

"When Jillianna refused to enter the church, Father Green agreed to perform the exorcism in his office. However, when he sprinkled holy water over Jillianna's head to begin the ritual, she began to age until she dissolved into a heap of dust. I watched her spirit rise up from the dust. I was feeling terrible, as though I had betrayed her trust in telling her everything would be all right. But, you know, from the smile covering her face as she walked into the light, I am sure she is happy the way it all turned out."

"All right, I'm not making light of what happened to the Romanetti woman, but two things, I doubt you will need to worry about her coming into your dreams anymore to play footsy, Jack and too, if the good father can see that he was wrong about her being a vampire and that being touched by holy water could make her dissolve into a heap of dust, then he should be able to see that more is needed to rid this parish of Rougarous."

"You'd think," Jack agreed.

"I feel so much danger for Regina and Rayford. Knowing they were upstairs in bed while a young girl was being murdered in the basement will not stop weighing on my mind." Seelah shutters.

"We've talked 'til we've run outta things to say to make them leave that house. They won't listen."

"I hate to say it, but until one or both of them are murdered in that house, they will continue to ignore us."

"I agree with you, Donavan. I'll tell ya if I didn't have a family I'm responsible for, I'd wait til` they're gone one day, and I'd go over there and blow that whole goddamn place clean off its foundation, again."

"And I'd be right beside you, Jack."

"I have an idea," Barb speaks up. "Why don't we ask the priest if he would be kind enough to talk with Regina and Rayford about what he himself witnessed concerning Jillianna Romanitti?"

"I think that is a great idea, Hon. In fact, I think it is such a great idea. I am going to call him and see if he will be willing to meet us out at the Hindel Estate later this evening. And speaking of the Romanitti woman, I need to send a couple of deputies over to her mansion to tell Baxter she won't be coming home."

The chilling scream echoed through the house, bringing all who heard it to their feet.

"Donnie!" Jack yells, running down the hall, his gun already cocked and ready.

Jack flips on the bedroom light and is shocked at what he sees.

Seelah runs past him and into the room, going to Donnie, who, surprisingly, is fast asleep.

"What the hell's goin' on? We all heard that fuckin'

scream!"

"It was a warning, Jack. A warning that they are coming for Donnie," Seelah whispers.

CHAPTER 33

"Regina, you're gonna have company any minute, and I want you to be prepared. I've already opened the gate."

"After all that has been going on here, I am not in the mood for anyone to visit. Not detectives, or priests and I am for sure not in the mood to see Jillianna Romanetti."

"There's a welcome surprise." Rayford laughs. "I thought you and her were best buddies."

"That has all changed. I do not care to be friends with a woman who not only believes herself to be a vampire but who also believes me to be her long-lost daughter from a past life."

"Hmm, she is even crazier than I thought."

"Yes, she is not mentally healthy. However, as strange as it may be, I do miss her. She has the qualities I look for in a person I can spend time with."

Regina gets to her feet to walk into the kitchen. Rayford follows her with his arm around her trim waist.

"I am going to pour myself a glass of wine. Would you like something? You still have a six-pack of beer in the refrigerator." She closes her eyes, shaking her head.

"I know, but I think I need something a little more bracing than a bottle of beer." He lifts an almost full bottle of Scotch, sitting on the large island atop the blue-green quartz countertop and, taking a glass from the cupboard, pours a hefty amount into the glass.

Seated on a long white leather couch with their feet propped up on a wide footstool, Regina turns her attention to the handsome man sitting beside her.

"You haven't told me who is coming for a visit."

Rayford gets to his feet as the door chimes announce a visitor.

"I think I will let you see for yourself," he tells her over his shoulder.

Rayford opens the door to see Donavan and Jack accompanied by Father Green and a pretty and young, black girl.

"Come in," he stands back to allow them to enter the house. "I was just tellin' Regina we're gonna have company this evenin'."

Regina remains seated as the young girl looks around the room.

"Someday, I will have a beautiful house just like this," she whispers.

"My name is Regina Hindel, and I am the owner of this house. And what is your name?"

"Gina Hastings," she says in a whispery voice.

"Are your parents prominent in the parish, Gina?" Rayford asks.

"No," She shakes her head back and forth. "Me and my mama and daddy live in the bayous. We ain't got no money and sometimes we ain't even got food to eat. But soon, we's gonna have everything we ever wanted." She giggles a high-pitched laugh.

"Gina," Father Green holds out his hand, "you need to

come over here with me."

Without a word, the strange acting girl walks over and quietly takes hold of his hand.

Rayford turns. His voice is low as he speaks quietly to Jack and Donavan. "What's wrong with that girl? She acts like she's fucked up on drugs."

"It's worse than drugs," Donavan says. "Father Green brought her along so she can tell us what is going on."

"Father Green hinted at what will be said and wants us to hear this for ourselves, as he believes the girl to be in danger," Jack speaks up.

"He sure is getting a lesson in the evil goings-on in the parish here of late." Donavan laughs slightly.

"He's gettin' a lesson in what it means to be a priest," Jack replies.

"Everyone pick a place to sit and get comfortable," Rayford tells them.

"Rayford, I would like for you to come back and sit with me after we find out if anyone would like a drink," Regina says.

"Donavan and I'll take a double shot of whiskey. Father Green?"

"Yes, I'll have the same. Thank you."

"All right now," Rayford hands a can of soda to Gina, "I guess we can get on with finding out the latest goings-on in the parish, and since we are all gathered here in the mansion, I think it is a safe bet the Hindel Estate is somehow involved."

"I would like for Gina to tell all of you what is going on in her young life at this time," Father Green said, leading Gina gently across the floor to seat them both in the deep green chairs sitting side by side near the white leather couch where Regina and Rayford are seated.

"I really do not care to hear any more parish folklore about my home or about my family, so if this is what you have in mind, then all of you can take your leave right now."

"Ms. Hindel," Father Green speaks up, "there is not one of you who would rather not hear anything about this house more than me. But, the time has come when we have to put our own wants aside and listen to what a young girl, whose very life may be in danger, has to say about your home."

"I said," Regina begins only to be stopped by a calming hand on her shoulder.

"Regina, I think you should stay quiet and listen to what needs to be said here. I doubt a man of the cloth is going to be the bearer of silly rumors." Rayford sits forward on the couch to stare over at her.

She looks at him, then leans her head back against the couch and closes her eyes.

"A few days ago, Gina came into the church to say a prayer. I was in the church at the time, and I came and sat down beside her to see if she might need my help."

Gina nods her head and takes his hand to hold tightly in her own.

"Gina told me that very soon she and her family were going to be very rich. Since I know they live in the bayous, I asked her how I believed this would happen. I will let Gina tell you what she told me."

"My mama said I would finally be able to do somethin' to make my kinfolk proud ah me. My mama ain't never had much use for me since she got herself pregnant with me from another man. A white man at that. She said if I don't do what she says, that I will have to start bein' a ho like my sisters."

"How old are you, Gina?" Donavan speaks up.

"I be almost fourteen."

"Are your sisters a lot older than you?"

"Yeah, they be grown womens."

"Okay, go ahead and tell us what your mama said you had to do to make the family rich."

"Mama said that we can all be rich'n all I gotta do's give my soul to da devil," Gena whispers. "Father, I don't wanna give my soul to da devil. He bes evil."

"Don't you worry about anything, Gina. You will not have to give your soul to the devil." Father Green places a comforting arm around her shoulders.

"How did your mama say you was gonna be able to do this? Is the devil supposed to come to your house?" Jack says.

"No. She said a man would bring me here to dis house. Dat there'd be a ceremony, and that's when I'd tell da devil he can take my soul."

"Did she actually say the house you would come to is the Hindel Mansion?" Donavan asked her.

"Yes, she says de Hindel Mansion. She said after I gives my soul to the da devil, then we'd all be rich, and my sisters could stop bein' hos."

"When were you supposed to be in this ceremony here at this house?"

Last Sunday. But nobody come to get me. I's happy all dat day, 'cause I thought it was all just 'nother silly game da was playin' on me."

"They didn't need her that night as they already had Jennifer Teals," Jack said, looking at Donavan.

"Thank you, Gina. You have been a very brave young lady to tell all of this to us. You won't be going back to your mama. You will be coming with Detective Olivier' and I to a house where good people will keep you safe. We'll let your mama know that you won't be coming back to her."

Regina leans forward on the couch. "I am sorry you have been treated so badly, Gina. But I can promise you, no one at this house will ever hurt you."

"I hope you will be able to keep that promise, Ms. Hindel," Jack tells her.

"Now, as much as I hate to be the bearer of more bad news, I do have something else to relate." He turns in his chair to look over at Regina. "Ms. Hindel, I was told by Detective Olivier' that you are a good friend of Jillianna Romanitti. Is this true?" Father Green asks her.

"I did consider her my friend, but she has been saying things that I really cannot agree with or believe in."

"Can I ask you what it is she told you that you cannot believe in?"

"I really don't like to speak ill of someone behind their back. Let's simply say it was so completely out of the realm of being true that I think it is better that I end our relationship."

"Does this have anything to do with her believing that she is a two hundred year old vampire?"

"Dat can't be. Der ain't no such thing as ah vampire!" Gina moves over closer to the man seated beside her.

Father Green pats Gina gently on her shoulder and then turns his attention back to Regina.

"Ms. Hindel, as you know, I am a priest, and I am not given to believing in silly fantasies. But I am here to tell you that whether Jillianna Romanitti was, in fact, a vampire, she was something otherworldly, for she came to me for an exorcism to rid her of what she believed was making her unclean. From the mere touch of her hand, my own hand along with hers was badly burned."

"She must have had something in her hand you didn't see for her to do that." Regina sits up straighter on the couch.

"Then tell me how she was able to dissipate into a pile of dust when I sprinkled her head with holy water in readiness for performing the exorcism?"

"Oh my God," Regina whispers, covering her mouth with her hand.

"What in the hell is goin' on in this parish?" Rayford pulls a weeping Regina into his arms.

"I wish I knew. I know that demons can enter into a human and possess them. So I guess with that being said, it is not out of the realm of possibilities for anything else from the dark side to make themselves known."

CHAPTER 34

Seelah sits straight up in bed then swings her legs over the side to get to her feet. "Jack, wake up. We have visitors." She shakes him gently.

Without a word, Jack gets out of bed and reaches for his 38 in the small alcove above his pillows. Laying the gun on the bed, he pulls on his pajama bottoms.

"I am going to go get Donnie. He needs to be with us." She slips a robe over her nightgown before walking down the hall to Donny's room.

Jack moves silently from the bedroom and out into the hall on his way to the front room. "Come get some, you devil lovin' bastards," he whispers. "I'll fill your furry asses so full of lead that even your black-hearted demon from hell won't be able to put you back together."

"Daddy," Donny murmurs, taking hold of his dad's hand as Seelah holds him safely in her arms, "monsters were looking in my window."

"Don't you worry 'bout anythin', Son; daddy won't let anyone hurt you or Mama."

"I'm going to call on White Spirits. With this much evil, we can use all the help we can get."

"You do what you think's best, Darlin'." Jack reaches on the top shelf of the china closet and pulls out boxes of 38 shells, laying the boxes on the table, then picks up his cell phone.

"Donny and I will sit over here on the couch," Seelah tells him.

"Hello, are you here to protect us from the monsters?"

Glowing faces of misty figures break into a bright smile upon hearing Donny's words.

"We are protected, Donny. You don't have to worry. God and the Holy Light will always be stronger than evil," his mother tells him, dropping a light kiss atop his dark head.

Jack quickly gets dispatch on the line. "Yeah, this is Olivier'. I need about five cars complete with dogs at my residence right now. We are being surrounded by what I would guess to be Rougarous, and if you laugh at what I just said, your ass will be mine the next time we meet. To be on the safe side, you need to send a few cars with dogs to Hay's residence."

"That was a good idea to send backup to Donavan and his family, too, Jack."

"Yeah, now I need to let him know what to expect." He punches in Donavan's number then waits. "Yeah, man, sorry to wake you, but you need to know, deputies, complete with dogs, are en route to your house. We're surrounded here, and we can bet they're Rougarous. Donny said he saw monsters lookin' in his window. Okay, I need to have my hands free, so I'll talk with ya later, partner."

Eerie howls split the air from all sides of the dwelling. The deep guttural sounds making all in the house look around to be sure they are still alone.

"I will not allow evil to touch you or your family, Jack," a familiar voice speaks up.

The breath catches in his throat as he sees the one promising him and his loved ones protection.

"Chandra," he whispers her name as he moves forward.

Chandra moves slowly into his outstretched arms. "I will never allow evil to touch you or yours, Jack, as long as I can prevent it."

"You are always here when I need you, Chandra." Jack holds her close for a moment.

Chandra moves away to go to Seelah and Donnie.

They hear a loud banging on the front door.

Jack goes to the door with his gun cocked and ready. "Who is it?" he calls out.

"Backup's here, Jack." Comes his quick reply.

Jack opens the door to allow them to enter when he sees a jeep pull up. Quickly, Donavan and his family get out of the vehicle and run inside.

"As you can see, we didn't take time to change out of our night clothes, and I already called backup to tell them to come here," Donavan says, as Barbara and Jenny go to sit on the couch with Seelah and Donny.

"They are really ugly, Jenny," Donnie takes hold of her hand. "They were looking in my bedroom window. I know I shouldn't be acting like a baby, but they really scared me."

"I know, Donnie," she whispers, pulling him close; "I've seen them before, too."

Seelah squeezes Donnie's shoulder when he makes ready to reply, shaking her head back and forth to tell him to drop the subject.

Donavan and Jack walk into the kitchen.

"You and I both know who it is that called this visit we're having tonight."

"Dick. Our aptly named piece of piss who killed Jennifer Teals.

"We know we can't kill them while they are in their monkey suits, but we can fill them with enough bullets that they will have to go to the ER to be treated, and since the department has to get a call when gunshots are involved we can get a pretty good idea who a lot of them are."

"I'd rather shoot their fuckin' heads off so they can't come back," Jack tells him. "And, as you recall, brass already gave us the go-ahead to do just that."

Donavan snickers as he pulls his handheld radio into position. "Yeah, this is Hays. I need about ten deputies along with two dogs inside the house."

"What's the plan, Partner?"

"The plan is to take the war to the enemy. I want to make sure we get as many as possible."

"Stay spread out through the house. They could try and come in anywhere," Donavan tells deputies as they walk through the door. "And also, make sure none of you come outside. The other deputies will be further out, so if something comes close to the house, we will know it is there to do harm, and it will be taken down."

Just as Donavan and Jack step out the back door, they hear a deep guttural growl nearby. Jack pulls up his 38 and fires off three rounds right into a dark shape standing at the end of the patio.

"You want to do harm to these families, you better be prepared to die tryin', you sons ah bitches!"

Donavan whirls to fire off multiple rounds from his 44

Magnum bringing loud screams into the surrounding area as something moves up behind him.

High-pitched yelps from one of the K9s make Donavan and Jack hurry their steps to the backyard. At the same time, they both aim and fire, dropping the tall, dark shape that had the dog by its neck. Free now of its captor, the K9 runs up to them, whining his fear of what had hold of him only moments earlier.

Jack runs a comforting hand over the dog's head. "It's all right, boy. He ain't in any shape to cause you any more harm."

The dog licks Jack's hand in gratitude.

"You will give us the boy, or you will all die," a voice speaks out in the darkness.

"Why don't you grow some balls and come over here and try and take him?" Jack challenges the one standing in the shadows.

"The father of all will not rest until he has the soul of every man, woman, and child in this parish. You cannot win in this fight, Jack Olivier'."

"I think I got a pretty good shot at winnin', Little Dick," Jack tells him as he walks towards the shadowed figure. "Let's see if you're man enough to face me."

A tall shape covered in short black fur walks into the glow of the porch light. "Our father, Satan, protector of all who lives to praise his name, will never let us be destroyed. Give your soul to the keeper of darkness and know what it is like to have all you have ever dreamed of placed at your feet. Only Satan can protect you and your family, Jack. Call out his name, so he knows you are ready to be protected by his touch."

"Naw, I'd rather call on the three trusty bullets I have in my 38." Jack squeezes the trigger. Smiling as he sees the tall figure fall back against the side of the house then slide to the floor of the patio.

"Stay back, Jack. Let's make sure this son of a bitch can't do any more harm." Donavan steps forward and empties his clip into the body of the figure lying on his back.

Jack and Donavan quickly reload as they hear screams coming to them from all directions.

"I just had a hell of a thought, Donavan. If these fuckers go to the ER, we could be putting each and every member of the staff in mortal danger. We can look at a severed head just as easy as we can an intact body."

Donavan stares over at him for a moment, then, with complete calm, begins shooting off the heads of those already lying on the ground.

"I'll take that as a yes," Jack laughs as he joins in on the dismembering.

Donavan keys his mike. "If any of you are too weak-kneed to shoot off the heads of those you've taken down, let me know, and I'll take care of the removals myself. With the help of Detective Olivier', of course."

The sounds of many gunshots can be heard throughout the area.

"I guess they got it handled." Jack grins.

"We need to be sure and keep the kids in the house in the morning until the deputies get all the heads and bodies picked up. That would be one hell of a thing for kids to see."

"I hear ya. I guess since you and yours are already here and dressed for bed, you might as well stay the night. You and Barb can take the guest room, and Jenny can take the couch."

"I'm not going to argue. After this fiasco, I'm ready to call it a night. The fur babies can go in and out the pet door, so we have that covered too."

CHAPTER 35

Regina turns over in bed and runs a hand over Rayford's chest. When there is no response, she gets out of bed to walk to the bathroom.

Not bothering to turn on the hall light, she moves across the room and opens the bathroom door to walk inside.

"Please help me," a female voice is heard to say in the darkness.

"What's wrong, Hon? Are you having a bad dream?" Rayford reaches out to pull Regina into his arms. "Where'd ya go?" He switches on the bedside lamp to find the room empty.

Getting out of bed, he moves down the hall to the front room. He turns on the lamp beside the couch then walks to the kitchen.

He hears the same female voice as he heard before, asking for his help.

"Regina, the middle of the night is not the time to play hide and seek. If you are in need of help, then show me where you are." His tone of voice is bordering on anger.

"Rayford, who are you talking to?" Regina walks into the

room.

"I'm talkin' to you. You keep askin' for my help, and when I try and help you, I can't find you."

"I think you are walking in your sleep, my love." She giggles, wrapping him in her arms. "I was in the bathroom, and I did not need any help."

"Will you help me?" A girl's voice interrupts the quiet.

"Oh my god, Rayford, someone is here," Regina whispers as she tightens her hold on him.

"Who are you?" Rayford calls out. "You need to show yourself!"

"I am right here. Can't you see me?" Her voice is filled with fear.

"I can't see anyone. What is your name?"

"My name is Jennifer Teals," she tells him. "Please don't let the monsters hurt me."

Rayford untangles himself from Regina's arms and runs to the kitchen, where he left his cell phone. He finds the number he has for Donavan Hays. When he hears Hays pick up on the other line, he whispers, "Thank God."

"Donavan, this is Rayford Seals. I'm sorry to wake you, but Regina and I need help. We have a girl here in the mansion who keeps asking us to help her. We can't see her, but she says her name is Jennifer Teals! So, either we're both batshit nuts, or we got a ghost."

"I wasn't asleep. Jack and I have been fighting Rougarous. Hold on a moment while I take the phone to Seelah. My family and I are spending the night here at Jack's house."

"Hello, Rayford. Donavan says you have a ghost asking for help?"

"Yes. She keeps asking us to protect her from the monsters.

I've never had anything like this happen in my life."

"It's all right. She won't hurt you. She doesn't know she is dead."

"Oh, Christ! I didn't need to hear that."

"Has she told you her name?"

"Yes. She said her name's Jennifer Teals."

"The girl who was murdered in your basement. Yes, it makes sense that she would linger there instead of going to the light."

"Well, can you get her out of here? I don't mind tellin' ya, she's got me scared shitless!"

"If you will do what I tell you, you may be able to send her to the other side."

"No! No, no, I don't wanna be interactin' with no ghost. Can't you come here to the mansion and do what you do to get her outta here?"

"Hold on, Rayford, and let me talk with Jack. I'm not going to make any promises, but if he says we can come there, then we will come, and I will see what I can do."

"Goddamn it, Rayford! It's two o'clock in the mornin'. I am ready to call it a night since we have to get up and go to work later this mornin'. Just tell the dead girl to go to the light!"

"I ain't messin' with no dead ghost! You're the one who said your wife's a psychic and can deal with this shit!"

Seelah takes the phone from Jack's hand. "Rayford, I will come and see what I can do. I'll be there in a little while." With that said, she turns off the cell.

"Seelah, you are not goin' to the Hindel Mansion alone! I forbid it!"

"I know I'm not." She smiles into his face. "You're going with me."

***

Regina walks down the hall to the bedroom to get dressed. She pulls a satin nightgown over her head and picks up her robe. "I think you will want to put on some clothes, my love. Although I enjoy seeing you in all your masculine beauty, I doubt our impending company will."

"Every time we turn around, something else is goin' on with this shithouse!" He yanks on a pair of jeans he had thrown over a chair the night before and then grabs a fresh tee-shirt out of a drawer. "How much longer are you gonna stay here?"

"This is my home, Rayford. I thought it was becoming your home, too." She stands looking at him.

"I don't consider a place filled with Rougarous and ghosts and whoever the hell else we might run into here, my home. I'm about ready to put a flame thrower to this place. At least it'd make all the demons feel at home."

"Don't you even think about destroying my property, Rayford." Regina whirls on him, her eyes filled with anger.

"You still don't believe there's evil here, do you? You just heard a ghost askin' for our help after she was murdered in your basement, and you still want to stick your head in the sand and pretend that all is roses and wine."

"We don't know that a ghost is really here. This could be a trick by someone who wants to scare us into selling this estate."

"Jennifer Teals. Are you still here wanting our help?" Rayford calls out into the silence.

"Yes. I am so afraid," she whispers.

"I rest my case," he says, throwing up his hands.

Knowing they can't go to bed, they sit together in the living room, awaiting the ones they hope can end another problem in the Hindel Mansion.

The sounds of a doorbell ringing brings Rayford to his feet.

Rayford pulls open the front door. "Thanks for comin', and I'm sorry for my anger earlier. This has me at my wit's end."

"Those not used to dealing with the other side usually do feel anger mixed with fear," Seelah tells him.

Rayford holds out a hand to Jack. "Thanks, man."

Jack shakes the hand being offered. "I had a hard time believin' in all this shit in the beginnin', too."

Not wanting to waste any time, Seelah calls out to the girl who is standing across the room, her clothes covered in blood.

"Jennifer Teals, I am a psychic, and I am here to help you."

The frightened girl runs forward to stand in front of Seelah. "Yes, please help me. I am so afraid."

"Jennifer, do you know that you are dead?"

"Oh no, I am not dead. See, I can feel my body, and you can see me. I was able to run away from the monsters."

"Jennifer," Seelah takes her hand, "You were not able to run away. Your spirit has left your body, and now you need to go home to the other side where your loved ones are waiting. Who has passed on in your family? I will call them to come here to take you home."

"My brother, Michael, died, but he was only six years old."

"That is all right. He can come for you. All those on the other side are thirty years old, but when you see them, they are the age that they were when they passed over. Jennifer, before you go, though, will you tell me who it was who killed you?"

"Dick Eldin. He was my boyfriend, and he told me if I didn't do what he said and give my soul to the dark side that he would not love me anymore. He will do the same thing to Cathy, the girl he is going with now," she tells Seelah, then cries out with her arms spread wide. "Michael!" She wraps him in her arms. "I

knew you would come and help me, little brother."
"Walk into the light, Jennifer and go with God."

CHAPTER 36

Thought you would like to know that the brass is giving both of us a medal for what we got done last night."

"Yeah, I think shootin' the heads off Rougarous calls for a medal. You shoulda suggested they throw in a free dinner to go along with it."

"They are. We will be getting the medal along with a dinner at the awards ceremony."

Jack walks behind his desk, leans his chair back and props his feet up on the desk. "Since neither of us has brought it up, 'bout what went down out at the Hindel Mansion, I guess it falls to me."

"What's there to say? You told me all that happened."

"Don't play dumb, Donavan. We're both askin' ourselves if what happened will have any effect on gettin' Regina and Rayford the hell outta there."

"And my answer to that is no. She will still be running around with her head up her ass and telling herself none of what happened, happened."

"She even heard Jennifer Teals' voice. That right there

should be enough to send her scurrin' out the door."

"Until something actually grabs her by the throat and uses her for a sacrifice, she will continue to believe this is all parish folklore."

"That and she's protectin' the Hindel name. Speaking of names, I need to send over a deputy to warn Cathy to quit her job and get the hell away from the Eldins."

"No shit. She probably won't believe the warnin', but now that ole Dickless Jr. is no longer among the livin', she needs to leave while she can."

"Good point."

"I been thinkin' I know Regina was my daughter in a past life, but somehow I still feel responsible for her well-bein'."

Donavan turns in his chair to give Jack his full attention. "Where are you going with this, Jack?"

"I think it's up to me to try'n get through to her 'bout what's goin' on in the mansion."

"Okay, and just how do you plan to do this without putting your own self in danger?"

"Simple, I'm gonna ask you and Barb to keep Donny at your house this evenin' while Seelah and me go to the mansion."

"Does Seelah know about this big plan?"

"She will as soon as I call her and fill her in."

***

"Regina thought I better warn ya. Jack Olivier' called me earlier and said he and his wife are comin' over later this evenin'."

"Rayford, why do you insist on bringing these weirdos to my home? I have told you over and over I do not want anything to do with such people."

"I keep bringin' them because I keep hopin' you'll wake up and see that we're up to our ass in danger here."

Regina gets to her feet to walk to the portable bar. "I am so tired of listening to all the insults aimed at my family name. I don't believe them, and I will not tolerate them. In case you haven't noticed, this is still my home, Rayford, and you are still my hired help." She busies herself with pouring a glass of white wine.

"How the hell could I forget somethin' as important as that, Regina?" He moves across the room to the refrigerator to pull forth a bottle of beer. "I guess what we've been enjoyin' these past nights is just what's referred to as fringe benefits."

"There is no need for you to get vulgar, Rayford. Just because you're my lover does not lessen the fact that you are still my hired hand."

Rayford slams his bottle of beer down on the counter. "There's a better name for what I am to you, Regina. And since we're on the subject of me bein' just your hired hand, I think I should be gettin' paid for that title."

"Whatever are you talking about, Rayford?" She turns with her filled glass to walk back to her chair in the living room.

"It's called bein' your hired stud, Regina. And since you've let it be known that this is all I am to you, I will expect a few hundred bucks extra in my pay envelope this month. But trust me; I'll make sure I earn every penny!"

The ringing of the doorbell interrupted anything more either of them had to say on the, now, heated discussion.

"Come in." He stood back to allow Jack and Seelah to enter. "I do need to warn you, though. Regina is not in a welcomin' mood at the moment. But, since you drove all the way out here, I'm not about to turn you away."

Regina gets to her feet to come forward. "Rayford is right in saying I am not in a welcoming mood. As you already know, I do not hold with parish folklore or silly stories of ghosts and now the new fad, Rougarous. However, as you are now guests in my home, I will offer you something to drink and allow you to tell me why you are here."

Jack speaks up. "Yes, I'll have a double scotch on the rocks and what, dear, a glass of white wine?" His brows are lifted as he looks over at Seelah.

Seelah nods and holds out her hand to Regina. "Thank you for agreeing to hear us out, Regina. I am sure you were reared to believe that anything having to do with the paranormal is evil."

She smiles as she accepts the glass of wine Rayford hands to her. Then with Jack, she moves forward to sit down in one of the chairs in the front room.

"The members of my family were not church-going people. I was not raised to believe in God," Regina told them.

"I understand you are from New Orleans. Did you ever hear any stories of children being abducted or harmed?"

"Oh, you hear all kinds of silly stories. Since it didn't concern me, I never paid the stories any mind."

"Oh, there's a surprise," Rayford murmurs, earning him an angry glare from Regina.

"I am not trying to be rude, but can we get to the reason why you are here?" Regina looks pointedly at Seelah.

"The reason we are here this evening, Regina, is so I can prove to you that spirits really do exist."

"Are you saying you are going to show me a ghost?" Regina's voice has lost some of its in-control tone now.

Seelah smiles over at her. "No, I said I am going to prove to you that spirits exist. A ghost is someone who has not crossed over to the other side for one reason or another. A spirit is someone who has crossed over to the other side but can, at will, come back to visit. When the ghost of Jennifer Teals was taken home to the light by the spirit of her brother, you were unable to see Jennifer's ghost and the spirit of her brother. In order for you to believe what I am telling you, you need to actually see a spirit with your own eyes so you can no longer tell yourself that what you are seeing is simply someone playing a trick on you."

"I feel as though I have walked through the door of an insane asylum. And I have to tell you, I am not comfortable feeling this way in my own home."

"Fear of the unknown is very normal, Regina. However, in order to confront what is going on in your home, you first have to know the threat is real."

Regina is surprised to have Rayford walk over and seat himself on the couch beside her. "You don't need to be afraid, Regina. I won't let anyone or anything harm you."

Jack smiles, giving Rayford a thumbs up.

"Some years ago, there was a black woman named Chandra who lived in the bayous. Chandra was not only a powerful psychic but also a healer. All the blacks in the bayous would come to receive a psychic reading, or if they had a medical problem, she would heal them. "

"I am not interested in hearing about some old black fortune teller who claimed to be a doctor." Regina puts her face in her hands.

"Let me stop you right there, Regina." Jack glares at her. "Chandra was not some old black woman who thought she was a psychic or who thought she was a doctor. Chandra was a powerful psychic and a powerful healer and a beautiful woman I loved with all my heart."

Seelah smiles at Jack.

"All right, and just how does this powerful woman involve

me?"

"Some decades ago, the Hindel Mansion was owned by a man named Jonathan Hindel. From all I have heard, Jonathan was a very handsome man who was in love with a beautiful quadroon named Angelia, who was a psychic healer. When Angelia's father refused to allow Jonathan to buy Angelia, Jonathan took his revenge and killed the man who stood between him and the woman he loved. Later he was able to buy Angelia from the embittered wife of the man he had killed. Soon afterwards, Jonathan left New Orleans with Angelia to bring her here to the parish. And in a very daring move, he married her."

"Jonathan Hindel married a black woman?" Regina sits up straight on the couch. "Why in the world would he do such a thing? He could have used her as was the way back then since she was his property. But to actually give a black woman our name," she presses a hand against her chest, "as though she was as good as us is unheard of!"

"Jack," Seelah puts out her hand, "she is still a woman who needs to understand why some things happened."

"Regina, I'm doin' my best not to jerk you up'n slap the ever-lovin' hell out of you right now. So if you're smart, you'll keep your racist feelin's to yourself."

Jack turns to walk across the room then stops as he hears Rayford get to his feet. "And if you're smart, Seals, you'll sit your ass back down."

"I've warned you 'bout disrespectin' Regina. Either you apologize, or we can go outside and settle this once and for all."

"Set down'n shut the fuck up, Seals 'fore I show you up in front of your woman!"

"Enough!" Seelah gets to her feet. "There is too much at stake here for everyone to act like unruly children. Now I want both of you to sit down and behave as men."

When she was sure she would not be interrupted, Seelah continued with what she was saying.

"After they were married, everything went well until the night Angelia, unable to sleep, went for a walk on the grounds. Suddenly she heard the moans of a woman. She went to see what she could do to help and what she found was something only seen in someone's worst nightmare."

"What was it she saw?" Rayford asked, his voice little more than a whisper.

"She saw a monster bending over a young woman. Unable to stop herself, she began to scream. Her screams took the monster's attention away from the young woman, but now it was coming for her. Trying to silence her, it began to violently shake her until finally, the screams stopped. Early that next morning, Jonathan found his Angelia lying where, as the monster, he had left her. She was dead."

"Let me ask you, just how did you come to learn 'bout this story?" Rayford asked her.

"After Jonathan lost his Angelia, he found a woman who could take Angelia's place as far as being a psychic and a healer." Seelah ignores Rayford to continue with her story. "He also gave this woman another gift. A gift that allowed her to not only continue to live for hundreds of years on this earth but also to bring forth young girls from the bayou to house Angelia's spirit, thus allowing Jonathan to once again take his beautiful Angelia to his bed."

"You still haven't told us how you heard 'bout this story," Rayford said.

"I was told about the story from the woman who received Angelia's gifts. The woman whom I will now bring forth for you to meet."

Regina reaches for Rayford's hand and is glad when she feels his arm go around her shoulders to draw her near.

"Chandra, will you please come and be with us here in the mansion this evening?" Seelah's voice, as she invokes the presence of Chandra, is gentle and filled with feeling.

For a while, they sat in silence, sipping their drinks and waiting. Then a misty figure began to take shape in the middle of the room until a woman in a free-flowing white dress stood before them.

"Hello, Chandra," Seelah said. "We are so glad you can be with us here."

Jack walks across the floor, and holding out his arms, he brings Chandra close to him. "Thank you, Chandra. My daughter needs to know what she is up against here," he whispered.

"I will always come when you need me, Jack," she told him, running one hand down the side of his face.

"I don't how the hell you're pullin' this off, but I for one do not believe we're seein' a ghost."

"As I told you before, Chandra is not a ghost. She is a spirit who can come and go from this realm and back to the other side at will.

"Chandra, if you will please, tell us why Regina Hindel, now the owner of this estate and Rayford Seals, need to leave the mansion."

"The Hindel Mansion is filled with much evil. You can destroy the mansion, but the evil that has been present here for hundreds of years has seeped into the grounds of the estate. Just as the blood that has been spilled here can never be wiped away, for it is the blood of the innocent."

Without warning, white spirits began to appear, forming

a ring around the room.

"Do not be afraid. The white spirits are here for your protection. Jack," Chandra turned her attention across the room to where Jack sat beside Seelah, "the Rougarous that you and Donavan destroyed have come here to take their revenge on those living here. And, now that you are here, their anger is even stronger."

Low guttural growls filled the surrounding area, getting louder and louder.

Jack pulls Seelah close. "We need to do something. This is so loud it's damn near unbearable."

"Just stay quiet. I am glad this is happening, for it will show Regina and Rayford what they are up against by staying in the mansion."

Men carrying their severed heads move around the room, their shirts and pants soaked in blood.

Rayford jumps to his feet to run down the hall. Within moments he is back carrying a double-barreled shotgun. "Come on, you evil motherfuckers, you think you're gonna destroy us?" He fired off a round into the grotesque figures still moving around the room.

"Seals, you can't kill someone who's already dead!" Jack yelled over the growls and eerie screams being unleashed into the room.

Chandra turns to the white spirits standing nearby. "You will bind them in chains and take them to the dark side."

Instantly the headless figures are bound and removed from the room.

The silence is deafening.

"Now you see the difference between a ghost and a spirit." Chandra smiles at them.

"Regina, are you getting an idea of what is real and what isn't?" Jack says.

"This is so horrible that the human mind cannot even gather it all in," she murmurs.

"But you do see now that what we have been trying to tell you about the Hindel Mansion is true?"

"Yes." She wipes a hand beneath her eyes and, taking the box of tissues Rayford lifts from the end table, pulls some free to blow her nose. "Excuse me."

"It's all right. Blowing your nose is a human thing to do," Rayford tells her.

"So, now where do we go from here concerning the estate?" Jack speaks up. "After what you just witnessed with your own eyes, do you think it is safe to stay here, even for one more night and day?"

"You said that even the grounds are evil. So what can I do?"

"The only thing you can do is destroy the mansion and burn the grounds. I mean every inch of the grounds all the way to the water's edge. Then perhaps in a few years, you can sell the land and let someone else start over here."

"You can find another house. And if you like, you can buy land and have a house like this one built."

"What Seelah is sayin', Regina, is there are different ways you can go, but that the important thing is for you to leave here." Jack takes her hand in his.

"If you want, I will be here for you," Rayford turns her towards him.

"Yes, oh my god, yes, please don't leave me to go through all this alone. And please forget what I said to you earlier."

"You got it, but if you still feel like addin' a few extra bucks to my pay, I'll be much obliged." He gives her a roguish grin.

"Are you both going to stay here tonight?" Seelah asked.

"Yes. We will stay here tonight and get busy finding a house to buy later in the day. Seelah," Regina gets to her feet to take Seelah's hand in hers, "I want to thank you for coming here tonight and showing us what we need to do. And, although I never thought I would be thanking a spirit, I also thank you, Chandra."

Chandra smiles, and without another word, she disappears back into the light.

"We'll be goin'. I'm glad that now you see fit to remove yourselves from danger."

Rayford holds Regina close to his side as they see Jack and Seelah on their way.

CHAPTER 37

Chandra stands in the darkened living room of the Hindel Mansion; however, she is not alone in the room. The spirit of Jillianna Romanitti stands beside her.

"There is so much evil in this house that it cries out to be heard," Jillianna whispers.

"Jonathan Hindel, the man who lived in this house for many years, was introduced to evil by a man who was the epitome of evil and also his father, Rafael Hindel. Rafael lusted for the blood of the innocent. He believed it gave him power, and power is what he craved. He wanted to be just like Satan, the one he worshiped."

"I have only been home on the other side for a short while, but already I can see how everything is perfect. There is no pain, no crying and no hatred. There is only love and laughter."

"Why did you wait so long to be cleansed of being a vampire?"

"I did not know I could be cleansed. I knew I could not touch a man of the cloth or walk into the house of God. If I had not found Seelah, I would still be one of the unclean."

"Seelah is a good woman and much loved by our Holy Father. Even though she is aware of the love that exists between Jack and me, she still welcomes me with open arms."

"You were in love with Jack Olivier'?"

"Jack entered into my life while I was still a psychic healer. He pulled me from the darkness I had slipped into and taught me what it feels like to be a woman with normal desires, not the filth Jonathan Hindel introduced me to when I was still a young girl."

"I am glad you were able to find love, Chandra. Were you and Jack together long?"

"Not long enough. When Jonathan found I was in love with Jack, he threatened to destroy him and to tell Jack the secret I kept hidden."

"What was it you were afraid for Jack to know? If you loved each other, there should be no secrets. There should be only trust and truth."

"Not when the truth could destroy another person. Jonathan knew that my black blood would bring only shame to the son I bore. Lawrence Hindel would not be able to hold up his head if he knew his mother was a black woman. Even though I was a quadroon with but a small amount of black blood in my veins. Lawrence was so proud to be the son of Jonathan Hindel, the pillar of this parish. In the end, not only did Lawrence learn that I was his mother, but that Jonathan was not his father, the one thing that even Jonathan was not aware of."

"What a terrible life you must have led before you found Jack."

"In order to keep Jack safe, I had to keep pushing him away, for if I didn't, Jonathan would have destroyed him."

"Now, here we stand side by side. Two women who love Jack Olivier'."

"When I learned about what you were doing coming into Jack's dreams at night, I wanted to stop you. But, because you were not evil, I was not able to interfere. There is a difference between being evil and being unclean. You were made unclean by a curse; you did not choose to be evil. And when you stopped hurting others to satisfy your blood hunger, you were becoming more worthy in the eyes of God."

The smile on Jillianna's face at hearing Chandra's words could not be hidden.

"When one chooses to return to God, no matter how dark they have allowed their soul to become, they are no longer able to make a decision that belongs only to God. We can, however, call on white spirits to remove dark entities."

"Now that Jack knows the soul of the child he and I had in a past life lives in the body of Regina Hindel, he tries to protect her even from herself. I am glad for this."

"This parody of darkness has now come full circle. Until this house is destroyed and the grounds on which it stands is burned, we will keep safe the one person who can end the Hindel Legacy. Rafael Hindel introduced evil into the Hindel Mansion, and now Regina Hindel will be the one to see to its demise."

Other books in this series....

ABOUT THE AUTHOR

Judith Ann McDowell is a novelist and a screenwriter with eight finished novels and eight finished screenplays: Born in Devertown, Ohio, to Elwin and Laura McDowell, she is the youngest of five children.

World Castle Publishing, a new and fast-growing publishing house, first published Judith in 2011.

Judith wrote her first novel after a very vivid dream of a young reincarnated Blackfeet girl named Tia. The book titled Long Ago Memories is set in 1921 in Montana but soon takes the reader back in time to the year 1872. Following Long Ago Memories, the prequel to this story titled Fated Memories was written, allowing the reader to delve into the lives of Tia's parents.

Judith's first published novel, titled Rougarou, tells the story of Jonathan Hindel, a pillar of Saint Anthony Parish, Louisiana, and a werewolf. Set in a series, the books are titled, Rougarou, *Rougarou II, Rougarou III The Devil's Child* and *Rougarou IV Shadows of The Past. Rougarou III, The Devil's Child,* was endorsed by Ann Rule, the bestselling true-crime writer.

Judith is the mother of five sons, Guy and David and Rhett and Nick and William Lobie and lives in the Pacific Northwest with her husband Darrell and Chi, Varga, Isis, and Lacy.

Judith is, at present, working on her next novel.

www.ingramcontent.com/pod-product-compliance
Lightning Source LLC
Chambersburg PA
CBHW030136180626
46812CB00002B/712